Cate McGowan's wri[...] full of emotion that t[...] more but also comfor[...] are stories of powerfu[...] [...]ice, exploring the human condition in all its beauty and ugliness and everything in between. *True Places Never Are* introduces us to a major new voice in American fiction.

—Silas House, author of *Eli the Good*

Cate McGowan's debut story collection, *True Places Never Are,* travels nimbly through geography and time, taking us through cities of the past and present via timeless rural towns. Here, we encounter the fullness of human existence distilled into moments of elemental violence, thwarted artistic ambition, and palpable yearning for true connection—with family, lovers, and the land.

—Wendy Rawlings, author of *The Agnostics*

Whether she's writing about a farm boy's altercation with an irrigation machine, a female prisoner, or a fictional French Dadaist (in what is truly a tour de force), Cate McGowan's stories have all of the ferocity and precision of her fellow Georgian, Flannery O'Connor, but McGowan is more compassionate. And more hip. I felt the same sense of excitement about the variety and heart in this collection as I did, many years ago, reading Jayne Anne Phillips' *Black Tickets. True Places Never Are* is an impressive debut.

—Robin Lippincott, author of *In the Meantime*

Cate McGowan's first collection of stories, *True Places Never Are*, is a virtuosity of language and storytelling suffused with grace and wisdom. Her range of narrative appears limitless, her vantage point sublime and sensuous, earthy yet ethereal. Each story is jeweled and brutally rich with joy and sorrow. Possessed of an eye fierce for truth and a passionate empathy for the human condition, Cate McGowan gives us, in *True Places Never Are*, a stunning debut collection, a literary treasury of tragedy, honor, and hope.

—Melissa Pritchard, author of *Disappearing Ingenue: The Misadventures of Eleanor Stoddard*

True Places Never Are is a wonder. Cate McGowan is one of my favorite new writers.

—Kyle Minor, author of *Praying Drunk*

This collection of stories lives up to its title in that they take us deftly to true places we have never been, places that we get to know through cunning observation and beautiful prose. With Cate McGowan as our gracious and expert guide, showing us just what to look for, we come away enlightened and delighted for having made the journey through time to these places that feel both happily, and sometimes painfully, familiar. This book is armchair travel at its very very best.

—James Thomas, editor of *Flash Fiction International*

TRUE PLACES NEVER ARE

True
Places

Cate McGowan

Never
Are

Stories

MOON CITY PRESS
Department of English
Missouri State University
901 South National Avenue
Springfield, Missouri 65897

First Edition
Copyright © 2015 by Cate McGowan
All rights reserved.
Published by Moon City Press, Springfield, Missouri, USA, in 2015

Library of Congress Cataloging-in-Publication Data

McGowan, Cate, 1966–
True places never are/Cate McGowan

2015935544

Further Library of Congress information is available upon request.

ISBN-10: 0-913785-58-X
ISBN-13: 978-0-913785-58-4

Cover art: *Head Over Heels* by Gregory Eltringham, oil on canvas, 37 inches x 22 inches, 2005

Text edited by Karen Craigo & Michael Czyzniejewski
Cover and interior designed by Charli Barnes

Manufactured in the United States of America

www.mooncitypress.com

For my mother, who expected me to ask questions, yet love unconditionally. For my artist grandmother, who showed me a thousand shades of green in the tree tops. For my brother and sister, who were my first friends. For my teachers, human and animal, who encouraged my spirit.

And, for Bill, my husband and best friend, who is my true place.

Contents

ACKNOWLEDGMENTS

- "Arm, Clean Off" appeared in *Glimmer Train*
- "Everything's Lighter in Water" and "How Can You Title Longing?" appeared in *The Louisville Review*
- "Let Go" appeared in *Moon City Review*
- "In the Yard" appeared in *The Sunday Reader* in the *Raleigh News & Observer*
- "While Doing My Hand-Washables on Wednesday" appeared in the *Snake Nation Review*
- "Come to Me" appeared in *Tank Magazine*
- "It's Not Your Hat" appeared in *Vestal Review*
- "Lie to Yourself" appeared in *WordSmitten Quarterly Journal*

"Arm, Clean Off" was reprinted in W.W. Norton's *Flash Fiction International*

About the story "How Can You Title Longing?": The poet, Violet Gray Witherspoon (and her book, *Lest You Forget: The Poems of Violet Witherspoon,* published by Ardmore Publishing Company, Atlanta) are real entities. Excerpts from Witherspoon's poems are used by permission. All other information in this story is purely fictional. The publisher has provided a release.

It is not down in any map; true places never are.

—Herman Melville

Some places speak distinctly. Certain dank gardens cry aloud for a murder; certain old houses demand to be haunted; certain coasts are set apart for shipwrecks.

—Robert Louis Stevenson

PART I

AND I MADE A RURAL PEN

The country rooster does not crow in the town.

—African Swahili Proverb

And I made a rural pen,
And I stained the water clear,
And I wrote my happy songs
Every child may joy to hear.

—William Blake

If found dead ship express collect to Coleman Parrum, Corinth, Georgia … P.S. Stay where you are. Don't let them talk you into coming up here. It's no kind of place.

—from "Judgment Day" by Flannery O'Connor

Arm, Clean Off

The irrigation machine took it, slashed his arm off, a thick gash and a click of bones as it sliced right through. He'd dropped the wrench, reached into the engine to retrieve it. His dad had always said not to, but who would know? No one was around. Sweet-smelling alfalfa grass swayed with a rushing sound, skeins of dry waves danced in rhythm to the pulsing hoses. And the long arm of the irrigation machine spewed water in spasms, its wheels rolling by him like a slow locomotive, oblivious to his crisis, a grinding mechanism, craning over a fourteen-year-old.

It had all happened in a split second. He'd been distracted by a spotted hawk swooping down on a squirrel; he was stretching his arm for that wrench he'd dropped, a little farther—there, there at the tips of his fingers. And then he'd looked down from the hawk just in time to watch the fan chew at his arm, like in the movies, as if it were happening to someone else, no time to snatch it out of harm's way. The fan blades had cut his left arm, clean off. Just above the elbow.

He took a header off the top of the engine, into the wet field, green clumps swallowing him up. Blood was gushing now. He licked the salty corners of his mouth, stared up into the blue sky above, and saw red on the plants where he'd toppled, little purple buds on the grass there. He lay back, thinking through the pain to shape a plan. *I'm not dead yet, no, no; that thump under my eyes is my heart.*

Down the slope, he could see the farmhouse and the creek. He was alone—it was Saturday morning. He'd been left to work; they were all in town shopping. No one could hear him call. The field was empty, even—only the fierce, excited din of birds and bugs from all sides, the occasional bark of a dog from a distant farm. *I can lie here or get up,* he thought, blinking his eyes to dispel the dizziness. *I'll lie here a second. I'll catch my breath. That blue sky overhead, the clouds all crisscrossing, is a big stadium, a broad net. Other people have emergencies; everybody does. Everybody takes a look up at the sky sometimes, faces it.* He thought of those people in other places, lying in rocky soil, watching the same sky, too. Beautiful girls pouting in parks, kids homesick at camp. Flat on their backs.

The cut decided on a dull throb, which droned in tempo to his pulse—"One-and-two-and ..., one-and-two-and ...." He reached his right hand over and felt something fleshy. His sleeve was torn. Mom wouldn't be too happy about that. He grabbed at something sticky over by his knee as he tried to sit up. It was his arm, the one that was cut off. He clutched it, covered in blood, to his chest, then set it down gingerly.

He'd seen tourniquets done in lots of Westerns. *A tourniquet'll save your life, son,* his dad had said long ago. The belt came off easy, even with one arm. Getting it around his torn biceps would be the hard part. He held the leather in his teeth and lay down to wiggle his new stub through the loop, then grabbed the end with his good hand and cinched it, then gripped it in his teeth again. Groping around, he found a thick twig left over from trees they'd felled last year, stuck it in the buckle, twisted it, tightened it over his wound, fastened it with the bandanna from around his neck. Blood was everywhere now; he swiped his gooey hand along the leg of his jeans.

He'd walk. With his arm. The field was spinning with the irrigation. Water was in his boots now. The dark, rich soil made an oozing, bubbling sound as he stepped. The tractor was parked a good ways off, maybe a half mile. Dad didn't like him to drive, but he'd have to now. His key ring jingled in his pocket as he walked. Up the hill, he knew he could make it, up the small hill through the trees. Dad had always stationed the John Deere under an oak, by the road, so it wouldn't get wet. *Out of reach of that damned machine,* his dad had said once. Now it was so far off.

His cutoff arm was dead weight, like a football cradled there, nestling in the crook of his right elbow; he touched the fingers. *How strange—it's asleep, yes, it needs some rest for the long journey. No sensations. It's waiting, waiting, tingling.*

He pushed ahead. One foot, then the other. He thought he was probably losing lots of blood. Water from the machine had collected on his eyebrows, trickled into his eyes. He couldn't chance swiping his good hand across his face—he might lose his precious package. It might spin down the hill. With the thought of his arm tumbling down the hill, he remembered the "poor meatball song" he'd learned at camp. "It rolled off the table and out through the door."

Dad is gonna be mad. I left that machine going full throttle.

He looked around him, tried to keep going. The day burst with changing light, and he walked in and out of cloud shadows. The shade volleyed back and forth, all purple and pink in the bright air, the morning sun reflected in the wet grass like shattered glass, and the field looked like an ocean, though he'd never seen one. Trees in the distance were dancing. Bent all together, the grass parted and there was a zigzagging pattern across the pasture where a groundhog was running. *Think through this,* he thought. *Ignore the throb.* Were all these sights real or not? No, no, he was sure he was walking, one step, then another, diagonally up the long, sloping tract.

I am walking toward help, he thought, *with the grass moving like water, and there's no one. Got to reach the pine woods.* Two fields down a ways was the house; waiting, vacant, and off to his left, hidden by trees, and almost out of sight, was the John Deere for which his dad had outbid everyone at the co-op. Up through the clearing he stumbled, leaving the field, stepping between two crab apple trees. He found the path easily enough.

He made it to the tractor. And there, a crow, no, two, perched on the steering wheel. They took off reluctantly with a brush of wings only as he charged them. "You ain't gettin' my arm!" he screamed after them, remembering the times he'd seen crows pecking roadkill.

It was a hard start, the tractor, especially when it was cold. Always had been. But the pine trees hadn't been shading it all morning, so he knew it was warm enough. He gripped his cutoff arm on the seat between his knees, twisted his tourniquet, tightened it a little, then gunned the engine. A breeze, tinged with the sweet smell of fresh manure, blew in from the Potters' property. That's it. That's where he'd go.

He U-turned; easy enough with one arm, but the spots in his eyes were big. Everything was getting foggy, zooming inwards. *No,* he blinked hard. *I'm not going to pass out.* And before he could blink again to clear his eyes, there was a pine looming large in front of him. He'd pulled the clutch out too late; the tractor had stalled, the bumper wedging between a stump and a tree. He turned the key a few times—it was flooded.

He pried his arm from between his knees, the fingers dangling lifeless, and he saw dirt on the hand like it was some other kid's. He touched the full crescent on the thumbnail. It was cold.

He headed for the creek: His dad kept a truck for towing logs down there in the ravine, off the old farm road. *Only a few more steps. I wonder if I'm leaving a trail of blood.*

A flurry of gnats swarmed in his face, around his wound. He ducked wildly to avoid them. A breathless symphony of cicadas, bullfrogs played on all sides. Raw, melancholy calls of crows—*Caw! Caw! Caw!*—sang to him. A powerful heat rose from the ground, rushed up his body, into his face, down to the gash. The gnats seemed to disappear, but maybe he wasn't noticing them anymore.

What had his attention was the sky, all bleached out with a sickle moon. It looked so comfortable as it rested there on top of tree points, like a broken egg in a nest. Down the ravine he stumbled, the clay soil rucking up behind him. The bottle-green water trickled over pebbles and rocks in the stream.

The truck—*She's a good ol' truck,* Dad had always said—there she was. Down with the clutch, in with the key, it was getting hard to keep his eyes open now; he had to think in steps. The truck fired and started right up. His arm was on the seat beside him. *Did I put it there?*

He twisted the tourniquet again, then pulled the truck into gear with his only good hand. Only one turn to the Potters.

Out the road, he turned left, this time avoiding all trees. Now the pines were canopies for him, shielding him from the sun, like a tent or all those awnings they have in big cities. He was so thirsty. He'd find help.

The closest farm, the Potters. Just around the bend. He pulled up to their barn, the biggest in the county, then slid off the seat to the ground, reached up, and honked the horn. He couldn't cry out; his throat was too dry. The beating behind his eyelids had started to slow down.

Mrs. Potter appeared out of nowhere, her long legs in work pants, an apron around her waist; she stood there, her mouth spinning in a big orbit of orange lipstick as she hollered for her husband, for everybody.

I don't remember the truck being red, he thought, as he watched Mr. Potter run over with two farm hands. They crossed the yard in a hurry.

"Can I have a glass of water, please?" was the first thing he said. He hung his head, shielding his eyes from the slanting sun. Mr. Potter had on mismatched boots.

"My arm's in there." He pointed to his arm sitting alone and dirty on the truck seat, then turned to see Mr. Potter undo his own belt, yank it from his pants like a whip, and make a new tourniquet.

"This should help, son." Mr. Potter spun around to face his wife and spoke in a hushed tone. "Now, put that arm on ice and call nine-one-one. Let's get a blanket, and, for God's sake, call his parents." Mr. Potter turned back, twisted the tourniquet tight, and said, "We're gonna carry you to the porch, OK? Outta the sun. You'll be OK. I bet you get to ride in a helicopter or something." Mrs. Potter whisked the arm away. Two more Mexican workers ran from the barn and they fetched him up like a hog-tied goat. Someone was calling for aid from inside the house. He'd see his arm again. Maybe they could put it back on. *They have the technology.*

In a moment, Mrs. Potter was back beside him, her apron off.

"There're your parents; there they come right now, right on down the road." She pointed to his mom's car, broken taillights braking on the curve, turning off the main road. Mrs. Potter had little, glistening beads of sweat on her upper lip, in the fur there, when she held the glass for him to drink.

From the porch, he scanned past sparkling motes of sunlight to the long silhouette cutting all the way across the yard—the shadow of Mrs. Potter's legs was a huge pair of scissors as she stood there so still. His gaze then finally pushed far up where a cumulus cloud in the west formed a big hand, with the forefinger pointing down, like the famous picture he'd seen somewhere of God reaching to Adam. He knew he'd have to tell his parents what he'd done. They were going to be upset and mad, too. He'd tell them, *Don't cry, Mom. Dad, you stop your crying.*

WHEEL HORSE

It was blue twilight. Curtains of forest drew tightly around Jebediah Rucker's truck as he made his last turn onto the home road. He drew a slab of tobacco from his pocket, cut off a wedge, and pressed it into the leathery pouch of his cheek. The truck burst through the green gauze of the last stand of trees, and over to his left, grouped at the ridge of the hill, he spied the solemn silhouettes of his neighbor's mules. The cold had come early that October, and the mules bunched together, quiet creatures in the winter-bound air, their breath puffing out in a sad, dense fog, their black outlines skinnied against the dimming light as if they were a menagerie of shadow puppets— head, tail, head, tail, all lined up.

He sighed, averted his eyes from the sorrowful sight, rolled up his window, and shivered. That W.E. King. It was bad enough that he'd probably win the mule pull in a couple days, but Jeb's next-door neighbor didn't care a lick about the cold or how his own exiled mules suffered. Just last month, in the midst of a rare heat wave, he'd watched big, fat King let loose his snides on the lower fifty, a scraggy pasture that dipped into a flood plain. And while some of those poor equines were starving out there, King kept his competition winners fat and hunkered down in a new red barn. The man left his screws to fend for themselves. Over the weeks, Jeb watched as the poor outcasts' bellies pinched their backbones from hunger.

The truck mounted the last crest toward home. He gunned the engine as he passed the mules, and there was a knob in his throat. He swerved, downshifted, the moist clay on the shoulder gave in to the heft of his truck, and mud spray slapped his tailgate. Country logic had kept Jeb from acting the full way. The mules were King's problem. No overlap there for sure, but folks, even Jeb, were naturally inclined to do neighborly things—he had begun to check the mules' water trough every couple of days; he'd even started dropping off a few bales of feed with his tractor.

Now with early autumn dormancy, the mules' pasture was naked, and Jeb sensed the starving mules waited for him, waited for his rusty tractor to buzz up the property line. Those mornings when he fed them, he'd find the poor animals pushed up against the fence, gaping patiently as he sat high on the tractor's hard seat. While his tractor idled, he'd pull open the gate, then pull in the bales. Though they first stood detached, the mules eventually struggled forward, all skin and bones poking out, amber eyes shiny and watchful. It was a matter of trust—and desperation; they'd lower their heads to the bale and begin to eat, tearing furiously at the hay with their yellow teeth and curling their maroon tongues around the dry strands of alfalfa. When they were full up, they'd scuffle and stomp, nostrils and bellies swollen. Jeb could then go about his day with a bit of pride; he was saving something because he could.

Papa said they were "living glue, sure to die, don't waste nothing on 'em. Hear me? Nothing." And King would rather they starve. At some point, Jeb would call the county to report animal cruelty. There was no other way; he and Papa didn't have the resources. His grip tightened on the wheel and he turned into the dirt driveway.

Jeb Rucker, thirty-four, not a year older, six-foot-three, not an inch shorter, with a thickness to him, slammed the door of his cab, and stood in the big, round yard. Beyond the hill, there was the shimmer of light in his own trailer's windows. And beyond, the property line visibly cut through the thick of woods, separating their farm from the Kings'. Lines and fences were about all the two farms had in common. Jeb sighed again. He knew Papa was already sitting in his chair, waiting for him.

He breathed in the chill, chewed on his wad, kicked sawdust and lumps of manure, and gazed out at the clearing. It was all barren now; just last week the woods near the house had been deep with trees. Now, the west pines were gone, felled for good money. He and Papa had their own mules to feed; they had competition fees; they had a lot riding on the mule pull this week.

Jeb whistled out at the field, and Rufus, a big mutt, came trotting on up, wagging and shaking with delight.

"That's a good boy! Miss me, big boy?" Rufus ran in circles, yelping.

And then Jeb heard Papa. He was clanging on his cake pan up inside the house. Usually, the beckoning call's metallic pitch carried straight to the road. Tonight it was especially loud, even out by the truck—*Trang! Trang! Trang!* Papa had surely heard him pull in, had heard Rufus whining with delight; the old man was hungry right about now, but he could wait.

This was Jeb's favorite time of day. Birds saying goodnight to each other, the bugs waking up, the mules in the barn drowsy from work. This was his time—and early morning. His trailer was set far off, away from everything, and the inconvenience was a trade-off; he looked forward to the dawn walk to the house for water, dew jewelling up the grass and birds yanking up worms for breakfast.

Spitting out the last of his chew, Jeb made his way to the barn. Netty and Bo, Papa's mules, whinnied and lifted their heads at the sound of his familiar gait. He threw in some sweet feed, freshened the water, then scattered fresh hay onto the floor. This farm, once a working one, was dead now, scrubby as any deadening in the South. The fields had lost their rows of corn to scratching kudzu vines; the warped outbuildings from the last century were no better than good firewood. But they had a solid barn and good mules.

And there was red clay, so acidic now without lime treatments. No worthy plant could set down roots here. The dirt stained all of Jeb's clothes a dull orange; stains wouldn't even come out with a good bleaching and boiling on the stove. But he loved this piece of the map: its intricate sky, its flocks of small birds like playing cards thrown through the air, its faint road off the back that drifted toward a walled-in horizon. The sweet smell of decaying plants and teeming forest and seasons.

Jeb threw a piece of wood for Rufus, then pushed onto the fence rail and faced the front door of the big house. Papa could wait a few more minutes. The dog came on back, the stick pale, stripped and covered in slobber.

The cake pan's banging reached his ears again. It was louder—*Trang! Trang! Trang! Trang!* Out by the old smoke pit, he sat for a silent spell in the barley grass. The ground was hard from the early frost. Rufus came loping on up, big ears crooked, running back and forth, dropping sticks and pebbles and dead crickets at his feet.

They both listened to the wind as it carried rustling sounds of moths and bats flying low to the ground, a steady whisper around them. And, as dark descended, a dim mist of moths, crazy in flight, swarmed over the heads of plants, and the insect cloud moved towards the funnel of light from the house as if the Rucker home were sucking them all in.

Jeb reached up to snatch a moth between his two fingers, and its wings fanned dusty on his skin. He felt its little legs dance on his hand and remembered how, as a child, he'd tie floss around the legs of a beetle, capture it, watch it fly in circles until it broke free and disappeared into the sky. Beetles.

Just last summer, he and Papa—before the old man was blind all the way—sat on the screened porch, drank their beers, and watched the beetles invade the yard and fields beyond. The mules bayed in their barn, and he and Papa gazed at the green, shiny-backed insects as they flew, riotous over the ground and thick in the sky. Some got stuck, their prickly legs attaching to the screen on the porch.

"Why can't ya stick to something like that?" Papa asked, pointing to beetles adhered to the screen. Jeb looked away, up at the starry night filled with crazy flying bugs. He thought, and then responded.

"Looks like they don't know where they're going to me."

Tonight, Jeb sat and turned the moth over in his palm. It had been patient there on his hand for so long. He poked it with a fat finger, watched as it felt its way to the edge of his thumb, about to drop off, fluttering. Gently, he guided it back to the middle. There were birds out there, black-winged starlings swooping down in flocks, feeding on bugs. It wasn't safe. He cupped it between his two hands as if they were a silent tomb.

From a distance, the desperate clanging on the pan summoned him, louder, more insistent now. As he walked up to the house, he ran his fingers along fledgling shafts of grass and finally let the moth go. It flew along the top of the empty field, and a gigantic, glossy-winged bird dropped down. It ducked and pecked but missed the moth stealthing along. Jeb attached hope to that moth.

Up to the house, his feet struck the ground in a deliberate beat, steady and sure. The metal clanging was frantic now. *Trang! Traiiiing! Traiiiiing!* A sensation welled up, one he felt so often nowadays—the want to turn and run back through the grass to the warmth of his own trailer. He reached the porch steps, and the banging stopped. He was sure Papa heard his boots on the stoop.

Inside, Papa's outline came clear, his flat nose, his right hand drooped over the side of his lounge chair, the pan almost touching the floor. And then Papa clanged on the pan again, even louder and more demanding. *Baaaiiing! Traiiiing!* Jeb crossed in front of him, knelt down to stare into Papa's blank eyes, *Baaaiiing! Traiiiing!* He pried the wooden spoon from Papa's bony hand, spoke no words, and stared into Papa's blank eyes for a long time, then waited. Jeb was so close. He could smell the mix of all the old man's odors: soap and sweat and rotting gums and teeth. And Papa stared at the space over Jeb's shoulder, surely not seeing anything, and he frowned, breathed hard, as if banging on that pan had taken all the energy he could muster. Jeb stood up. He could turn right now and walk out the screen door and down the steps and never come back.

But he stayed put.

"You gonna fix my supper and bath, boy?"

"Yes, sir."

"Well, hurry on up; I'm hungry and I smell like a week of digging ditches."

☾

Garnett Rucker resented his son for a stretch, from the boy's birth until recent times. It wasn't Jeb's fault: a good kid, happy, smiling, never much trouble.

For spankings, he made Jeb go outside to pick a switch. If Jeb brought back a paltry thrasher, Garnett made him go on out and fetch another one three times as thick. Of course, the little brat would test him and then return with a fat stem almost as big around as a man's wrist. Garnett knew it was natural for a boy to get smart, but he used those big, impossible branches to spank the boy anyway; a lesson had to be learned, and he inflicted some mighty welts. The boy would limp for days.

Later, when the boy got older, Garnett devised an even better punishment. He made his son run the fence rails. Jeb had looked at Garnett with fear after all that. But he liked it that way—he had himself a boy living under his roof, someone with no responsibilities. He hadn't asked for a child, but he had use for one. He could use him when there was work to be done on the flooding streambed, when there were fields to be sown and fences to mend and livestock to feed and tag.

But those hollow looks Jeb had taken to as a child, he'd never lost them, even in his adult years. They now worried Garnett in his blindness, in his memories. Nowadays, try as he might, he couldn't shut out flashes of his son's haunted expression.

Worse now—he couldn't remember Jeb's adult face. And these days Jeb tended to him real nice: *How 'bout seconds on that beer? Papa, turn over now; let me scrub your back. You need anything else?* How could Garnett reconcile with that?

Jeb. All Garnett had to do was bang on the cake pan. Lately, he wasn't sure if there was a future for the boy: He'd heard the chain saws tear through the trees last week. No, there wasn't anything he looked forward to. And those poor mules on King's property over there were going to die a miserable death.

That goddamned King.

Garnett's resentment for King kept him company. The bad feelings went far back, to when he was eight, right after the Kings moved in next to the Rucker property after some Yankee realtor down in Atlanta had sold the land at a bargain price. Garnett's mama packed up a welcome basket, and, with a few women from the church circle, took it on over. Mama came back disgusted. *Those new neighbors, the Kings, they have a still, and what's more, they're living in filth!* His own tee-totaling papa didn't take kindly to moonshining.

That summer after the Kings moved in, Garnett was lucky to never come across W.E. But then came the first day of school. Garnett took the trail behind the house, all overgrown with honeysuckle and four o'clocks, hacking his way through with a stick.

As Garnett neared the school yard, something wet plopped onto his head. First, he thought it was a bug or a bird dropping its breakfast. Garnett looked up, and there, in a big oak, W.E. King sat blowing spitballs from a reed.

☾

After that, it only got worse. Their teacher, Miss Avis Gilmore, spent most of her time trying to set King straight over small infractions: King cheating at dodge ball, flicking gum into some girl's hair, cheating in algebra with the answers penned on his palm. After a while, all King's small, wrongful acts built up in Garnett; yes, he took them personally.

Years later, King went too far with Henrietta. They'd all just graduated from school, waited around that summer with nothing better to do. Garnett worked hard, morning to nightfall, preparing his very own plot for planting.

One day in mid-August, Polly Eden came shuffling up the path, kicking rocks, swinging her arms.

"You heard about King and Henrietta? Garnett, you hear?" Garnett pulled up on his shovel, tossed a rock, wiped his mouth on his sleeve.

"Whatcha talking about?" His cheeks were already burning.

"Oh, I just come from Henrietta's. She's over the moon. King brought her sunflowers—just like those!" She pointed to the edge of the woods, and in the bright sunshine, there was a distinct hole in his mother's cutting garden where she'd nursed a small patch of tall sunflowers. "They were holding hands, sitting up 'til late."

Garnett left Polly Eden standing there, giggling. He threw his shovel and stomped the whole way over to the Kings'. And, as he came around the house, he saw the King men trundling around the still in the back. W.E. leaned against a stump, his foot propped up, and Garnett bounded up to the big boy and struck.

"Stay away from her." He swung; W.E. ducked, then hooked back with a fist hard as stone. Garnett was out cold. He came to after someone ladled moonshine over his face. He walked home, defeated, eyes stinging, clothes and hair reeking of 180-proof, the echo of the Kings' laughter hitting him the whole way.

"Stupid boy."

Saturday morning, Jeb was late—he saw Papa had found his way early on. Even as blind as he was, the old man was mobile, could walk with his shoulder pushed up against the porch rails. Papa was good at counting bushes, leaning against the barn for direction. Jeb admired how he knew every notch and splinter on the property, how he knew every pebble, every dip in the dirt. Blindness would not slow Papa down, stubborn as his precious mules.

Jeb spat out his chew, then harnessed up Netty and Bo in the barn, brought them outside. Papa stood there, waiting in the field, his flannel shirt misbuttoned, the shirttail skewed all crooked, and his walleyes, once piercing, were now dull in the morning sunlight, an opaline blue fogged like a cobalt glass filled with milk. Papa, rough farmer's skin crinkling around his eyes as he scowled, guided a hard, blank stare in Jeb's direction. Blindness hadn't dimmed his meanness.

"You gonna lollygag 'round all morning?"

"No, sir, just slow today, I guess. Had to go feed King's mules."

"That dog meat's a waste a money."

Papa turned and patted Bo, who stood patiently next to him and spoke to Bo and Nettry with a sugary tone he reserved only for non-humans.

"That's my babies. You're gonna win it for me, ain't ya?" In turn, Papa whacked Bo's hind with an open hand, then caressed it. Both the mules snorted with excitement, their flanks twitching with love jitters. With animals, at least, Papa was a real sweet-talker.

Jeb had long ago accepted that the whole town had dismissed his chances at the mule pulls. In Dry Branch, everyone knew that the Ruckers had never won. But Jeb had a secret weapon this year: Bo and Netty were the best chance they'd ever had against champion W.E. King. Jeb had trained hard for this. He was a good mule driver.

This past year, he'd gone to every pull in three states and seventeen counties, and he'd trained by entering and losing all the early competitions. He'd learned what worked by losing. So now, he figured he could learn by winning. Every driver he'd ever met, every veteran, was happy with advice. And now he knew how to push the animals hard but steady.

Jeb got down to business. He took a deep breath, inhaled the scents of fresh hay and sawdust and manure. And then, *Hupp-hupp!* The two mules strained and pulled their harness chains, stamping the dirt, waiting for a load, raring to go.

If Jeb squinted at the mules from a distance, they stood fine like horses, long legged and less stocky than most in these parts. Of the two beasts, Bo pulled slower but never gave up. He was a five-thirty coming up on six years old, what they called a wheel horse. Someone once explained to him that teamsters saddled wheel horses—the strongest, best animals—at the back of the lineup in front of the left wagon wheel. Wheel horses moved out first and bore the heaviest of a team's load.

Bo was a wheel horse all right, a big red sorrel, with a dark brown dewlap under his chin that wiggled when he moved. Netty was smaller and a mottled bay with short, pinched ears. Jeb loved her, too. Her kindness, her bright eyes with both lamps burning. She was one of those rare hinny types: her parents—some stud from down in Butts County and some good-tempered jenny—mated to make her one of the few mares in all the quad-counties.

And what was important, really, was that Netty kept ol' Bo happy. Just like a female should. She was calm, and, if she could talk, she would've never complained about anything. She turned a big, ringed eye on Jeb, nuzzled the palm of his hand with her wet nose. He knew he was never supposed to touch a mule's muzzle that way, but Netty didn't mind.

In the field, Jeb walked Papa to an old plastic chair by the log pile a good distance from all the mud. He sat Papa down, scooted the rain bucket close, gave him a metal cup of water to sip on. With the cup between Papa's knees, the old man drew his comb from his shirt pocket and dipped it in the water, then raked it through his long, white hair. Jeb smiled and Papa leaned into the big heap and waited; the mules chomped at their bits and waited, too—they were harnessed to the trace real taut, the sled slack weight behind them. Jeb breathed in the October air a second time, all rife with decaying leaves and sweetness. Poison ivy, a fierce red, was wilting at the eaves of the barn.

"Now, son, put those heavy logs on the sled. They gonna get some big weight." Papa pointed his cane toward the pile, looking like Mr. Spooney, Jeb's boss at the Piggly Wiggly, who sometimes aimed his pen the same way as he sat on the loading dock or at the front desk.

He handed Papa the mules' reins, then rolled each log from the stack onto the wide sled, and, as he pushed each one, he checked his slipping hands on the mossy bark, all wet and slimy. It took more than fifteen minutes to load up, and he was already tired. But Papa held the mules' reins tight and steady for him. By the time Jeb finished, the sled was heaving with logs; it held a massive load. It was kind of weight his mules liked.

They had all trained for months now; every night when he got home from his hauling job, he was out in the yard with the mules. They trained every weekend, every day off. They'd be pulling up to 5,500 pounds tomorrow. And in front of a big crowd. He didn't take chances.

He gripped the reins, pushed a shrill whistle through his teeth, and gave a *Hupp! Hupp! Huuppppp!* It was a slow start, but Bo and Netty dragged the sled clear across, sliding it through the mud as if it were slipping through warm syrup. His forearms were on fire.

"That's my good 'urns," Papa said as he listened at the smooth pull. He slapped his pointy knee and smiled, tapped his cane, rested his chin on his knobby grip, and stared off at nothing in the sky. The wind caught his hair; Jeb thought the old man looked like a big water bird. He let Bo and Netty linger, leaned against the fence rail, and looked down at Papa's head.

"I think they's ready," Papa said. "Course, logs ain't like those cinder blocks they use nowadays. I'm tired. You tired? Let's rest awhile."

"We just started, Papa."

"Well, I need a rest. Ain't like I used to be."

Papa would know all about the way things used to be. He'd always been harsh on Jeb—the worst licking Jeb remembered was when Papa made him run the fence line. He'd tagged the rails for ten hours. Must've been fourteen.

That day the light had glared, and he and Papa had worked all morning on a hayrack. After hammering the last nail, Jeb reversed the pickup out of the yard and into the field. With the new rack propped in the truck bed, Papa directed him, and Jeb watched from the rearview mirror, inched the truck back, his foot delicate on the clutch. But the clutch bucked, and the hayrack caught on the big limestone gatepost and slivered into splinters. It was ruined. Papa, face all red, commanded Jeb, pointing his finger at the long fence line that circled the huge farm.

"Move it, boy. Follow the line!" Papa's veins poked out on his forehead. Jeb did not hesitate. With terror in his legs, in his overalls and work boots, he ran; he scrambled along the fence, down the hill to the creek, over to the Kings', to the edge of the property, and back again, to the other side by the rising, over by the pine thicket and back again, past the hogs in their pen, past the mules chewing hay in the yard, past Mama, face all stony in sadness, as she set laundry out on the line. He ran the same path for hours.

Every few trips, he'd pitch forward and spit up bile and some creek water that he'd tried to slurp up fast. He started to see things double, sometimes triple, not sure where center was. But he kept running. Papa saw to that. At every approach, Papa cuffed Jeb on the head with a work glove, shouting, "Move along, boy. Move!"

Finally, at the tip end of that day, when Jeb's pants were stiff with piss and his feet were raw in his boots, when he gasped for water, when Papa left him to crawl the last lap, when the old man sat down to supper, it was Mama who came out the house and liberated Jeb. She pressed a cool towel to his face and offered him a cup. He drank for a good ten minutes.

Now, here he sat on the same fence line looking down at helpless, still-demanding Papa. All he could feel was the same wind that riffled the mules' manes. No anger, no sadness. None at all.

It would be tough going for Jeb tomorrow. Garnett wasn't sure if Jeb had ever listened to his advice, anyhow.

"Well, I need a rest. Ain't like I used to be." The boy dropped the reins in a clack of metal and leather, and the fence creaked with his son's weight. The boy gave up too easy.

He remembered the afternoon Jeb was born. The whole county had been dropping leaves for a couple months by then, waiting for winter's hunker-down, for the first hard frost. That long-ago day started out full of harvest. It was a day of composting and burning brush piles. And the stork delivered that afternoon.

Garnett should've been outside working, tending to his fields like every other farmer in the county. Instead, he stayed close to Henrietta. That same afternoon, King burned Garnett's most fertile field. Garnett had no proof, but he was sure it was King. He sat on the porch after Henrietta's labor screams finally drove him there. And what did he see? The beginnings of smoke, the first gray tufts. The horizon off the east smoldered bright orange. He knew he hadn't set it himself. He knew it could only be spiteful King.

That fire was their ruin. And it wouldn't have mattered so much any other year, but that summer, the east field yielded the most corn in the county, more than King's or any other farmer's for miles. Garnett hadn't tilled it under quite yet, believed what his papa had taught him—let the stalks dry and rot until first frost: They'd compost the soil to richness.

So that day, Garnett's first and only son was born, and his fields blazed. He ran out and watched fire swallow all those beautiful, composting stalks. The tinder-strewn field swirled like a large pyre, an undressing of sorts. He had never seen the ocean, but he imagined it would look like this, the ground combustion moving like water, for he had seen lakes and their heaves and whitecaps. Gone. It was all gone. That field wouldn't yield any more fat corn for at least two seasons. He had no rotation plan.

After that day, every time he laid eyes on his infant son, he pictured that fire, its dying embers, how its orange heat snapped and smiled at him. Garnett never really caught up after that, never had the money for Henrietta's doctors. Finally, he gave up, and, over the years, the fields had gone to rack and ruin and lay unplanted.

Now Garnett had gone blind in the space of six months, but Bo and Netty might bring some pride back to the place. Jeb had given him that. Funny, the fire wasn't on his mind as much these days.

Besides this land and Jeb, memories were all he had left. Henrietta would be sad to see where he sat, nothing to his name. She was what he'd really lost. This land and Jeb didn't mean nothing.

The first day he spent with her was the day they went into the woods. It was a simmering March Saturday—heat unusual so early in spring—and they drove down to the quarry.

Garnett woke early and finished his chores. And his buddy, Cyrus, had a pickup. Garnett sat in the back with a bunch of kids from school, and Henrietta was there, all beautiful and innocent. Sweet smells filled the air; blooming crab apple trees lined the road.

Above, the blue sky opened up as they sped through the countryside, and the swift air sang in Garnett's ears like an organ song. That day, Henrietta tied a yellow scarf in her hair, tight under her chin, and her brown eyes sparkled clear; her arched brows rose easily when she laughed. Every few minutes, she glanced at Garnett and tucked back strands of stray hair. The wind wrapped around her scarf, her blouse, her skirt like a caress. A couple times, when the wind tugged at her blouse buttons, he glimpsed her cream-colored undergarments. Garnett could make out her voice only when he turned his head in the whipping wind, when the breeze blew her silken words back to him.

Off the state highway, Cyrus steered the truck onto a dirt turnoff, the red clay a path worn smooth in two deep grooves. The high sun burned at the woods' rim, the shadows moved all darkly green, and a deep stand of pines settled around them, the thick woodland ablaze with wild purple azaleas. They went a ways until they hit a wet patch in the road, and when the truck pulled into the mud, it sunk deep, bogging down in ooze.

"All right, everybody out. Push." They piled out, Garnett, Henrietta, everyone. With a heave-ho and a spin of wheels, with Cyrus guiding the steering wheel up front, the mud pitched, and they finally rocked the old truck out, the wheels whirling, spraying a flume of muck onto Henrietta. Covered in mud from her elbows down, she looked as if she might cry. Garnett offered up kind words.

"It's OK. You can rinse those when we swim. It'll keep the mud from setting." He offered his elbow, and she pulled up out of the dirt. She used Garnett's shoulder for balance, but fell into him anyway. When she touched the skin just there under his shirtsleeve, it was like a flash, as if he'd suddenly come up on happiness, as if he'd surprised a butterfly in the woods. He had touched her arm a million times, but it had never felt like that before. He got a whiff of her hair, a faint, woody fragrance. Fresh sawdust in the sun.

"Not many boys know that kind of thing about stains, Garnett."

"Well, I'm not most." The quarry clearing wasn't far.

It was a crisp morning, perfect for a pull, and the Mule Day committee had hung large banners outside the stadium:

1825-1975, 150 YEARS! MULE PULL TODAY!

Inside the stands, from the bell-shaped speakers, the emcee's voice boomed onto the field and trickled out across the county's parking lots and side roads.

This was the start-up; the teams and their drivers shivered with excitement. But Jeb stayed steady and brushed down Netty and Bo for a third time. His mules felt no anxiety.

"And just to let ya'll know, this is Dry Branch's one hundred and fiftieth Mule Day. It's the oldest. It's the best. Over in the Shiloh High football field, we got a craft show going. And don't forget, our clowns are courtesy of the state rodeo comin' into town next week. Folks, drink and eat all ya'll can. Proceeds benefit the local Kiwanis and Dukey's Wayward Pets."

Jeb drew the short straw, would go last. So he watched and waited. Every team was as good as the next. The crowd's excitement pitched higher with each subsequent pull, and the emcee's voice pitched higher, too. And then it was Jeb's turn, the last team in round one. He made his way to the ring, there was applause, and he waited for the weight to be lifted on, then watched Bo and Netty's hinds go taut with the pull. He held on fast, tucked his right elbow under tight, and, as Bo and Netty shifted roughly, they skidded their front legs back and hauled with all their might, until he heard the emcee.

"That's how it's done, folks." Applause again, this time louder. The galvanized voice rattled the box speakers above his head. Jeb had cleared the first hurdle, pulled the qualifying weight.

It was already past noon, and, through his long, loose hair, the autumn sun beat down clear to his scalp. Bo and Netty were a little hot now, too, but they'd make it; those two were hard workers. As Bo pitched a little, Jeb steered them over to the side. He could tell they were excited from pulling that first weight so easily; they breathed hard, ears laid back, their flaring nares expanding then contracting. Netty's circled eye gazed at Jeb with confidence. He loosened his hold on the leather reins, unwrapped the straps from between his third and fourth fingers. He let the slack drag on the ground in a large flag loop.

"Son, get those mules some water!" Papa commanded from where he sat on the field behind the fence. Jeb nodded, though he knew Papa couldn't see.

Over by the stands, the clowns goofed off between pulls, mimicking the way mules pull a dray, hee-hawing and whinnying, exaggerating and huffing. One pedaled a purple miniature car in swirls, chasing and lassoing another whose Afro bobbled. The kids in the stands laughed and pointed, their mouths spread wide, their sticky faces pink from candy sticks.

W.E. King took the field after all the commotion. Jeb waited with Bo and Netty on the track; they were next. He checked the harnesses up on the tee, checked the dray. He leaned into Bo and Netty, heads hanging, patient. Jeb's chest was shaking. Now was when he'd have to push them. He paced. A cool wind gusted down and felt good.

King flicked his cracker whip and his mules were off, in unison, pushing their heads forward, leaning into their harness, pulling sideways with the easy effort. There was silence in the stands—respect, even. A baby cooed. A few tired bottoms shuffled in the hard wooden seats. King's mules hardly even struggled. They strutted, as if they were on a leisurely stroll, no strain at all. Then—"Aaahhhhh!" and thunderous applause erupted from the stands.

King's team had pulled that weight easy—3,500 pounds. Some teams were already disqualified, and this was an early round. He was sure Netty and Bo could match King, but Jeb was giving off a scared feeling, and he knew they smelled his fear.

☾

Old Garnett Rucker sat in a metal folding chair on the sidelines of the Dry Branch Mule Pull. It was a damn shame he couldn't compete. Sure, he was blind, but he could still get a job done. It was his boy he worried about. Course, Garnett wanted Jeb to win—anybody was better than King. So when Bo and Netty pulled off an easy 3,500, he started to think his kid had a chance.

"OK, next pull's W.E. King's. Folks, it looks like he's gonna add five hundred pounds. This here's a competition. Whoowee."

Jeb would have to fight hard now—but luck might have some part to play. Life, even its beginnings, was chance, after all. A breeze blew at his shirt collar, and he smelled what he thought was green water, and the memories flooded into him again.

That day with Henrietta at the quarry long ago—it was Cyrus, butt naked, who dove into the water first.

"That's cold." Garnett went along with the other boys down to his boxers and followed. He jumped in and felt the shock of winter water. Henrietta stood on the rock slab above, nervous, waiting.

"OK, y'all turn around. I'm gonna take these off and throw 'em in." She unbuttoned her muddy blouse and winked at Garnett, and the water radiated around him as if she had thrown a boulder by his shoulder. He swam into the middle of the deep and green quarry; the pale boys all paddled with their backs to the strippled edge. Garnett waited for the beautiful girl's splash, hoping at least for a glimpse of her reflection.

Later that evening, he and Henrietta would leave everyone; they would explore the woods. They found themselves keeping warm in a thorny bed of pine straw.

Eeeeee. The stadium's loudspeakers whined with feedback, brought Garnett back to the pull. "Sorry about that, folks. Sorry to say that Jaybird Olsen and Flip Spiceman just couldn't get it done. Give 'em a big hand. They had a bad day, but their mules don't know it. We're down to two—W.E. King and Jeb Rucker.

There was more clapping, and someone shouted in a throaty voice, "We love you, Jeb!"

"King's pulling now. Quiet, please."

Garnett's rear had gone numb from sitting, but he didn't care. He listened close, then heard a whip fracture the air. No sound of movement, no motion from the field. King's mules weren't budging. Garnett smiled, and the silent moment spanned forever, like leaves turned inside out waiting for rain. A woman's voice droned on up in the crowd, somewhere a loud whisper whiffled in the air, all querulous. Finally, a second snap of the whip and a grinding rumble on the field. And then the MC's voice cut through—"He's done it!"

Dammit. Garnett lobbed a ball of spit where he'd last heard King's whip. The crowd whistled and shouted and whooped. "All right!" "Way to go, W.E.!" The bastard's poor mules panted, snorting and choking on their own saliva. He could almost see their hard breathing, their sides like accordion bellows, heaving in and out.

Jeb was up. The forklift motored in from the sidelines once again.

"Looks like Jeb wants another two hundred fifty on top of King's weight." The emcee's voice cracked. Hundreds of eyes could watch what Garnett couldn't—what he would give to see his boy win! The forklift sputtered away, scraped over by the cinder block pile. A cough spumed from the back of the field, someone clearing their throat. Heavy feet clunked up and down the bleacher steps from the concession. And he heard Jeb snap the reins, and, with that, the clock started. Garnett counted to himself—*One Mississippi, two Mississippi* ....

Hupp-hupppp-hupp!

Nothing. Silence. No movement.

Hupp-hupp-hupppp!

Jeb pleaded with Bo and Netty. "Come on, you two!"

Hupp-hupp-hupp!

The stillness lasted way past twenty-Mississippi, there were only the sounds of Jeb's desperate appeals and Bo and Netty huffing and skidding their hooves and a cardinal somewhere far-off calling *purty-purty-purty, sweet-sweet-sweet,* and still no grinding sound. It spanned a lifetime.

Then, ever so slight, there was the low, telltale scrape and grind of a metal sled over dirt, the slight shake of earth as the force of Bo's and Netty's hooves dug in and found a hard place, and his son kept on chirping, almost a whisper now, *Heeupppp. Heeeupppp.* But then there was quiet again and the murmur of a prop plane in the sky. More scraping and hooves. A long hard grind and a stop.

☾

Who knew that in losing there could be such freedom? Bo and Netty trotted in front of him, tired, but still prime for more loads. There wasn't much sense in driving the pickup on such a fine night. And it wasn't a long walk home anyhow. Just enough light left over, too. He felt so wild and different now, as if something inside him had finally taken flight. The sky was big, wide open, not a cloud, but it burst in colors he'd never seen before.

His mules didn't care about losing, so why should he? Their gaits were still perky, their heads high with a springiness that comes with pride.

For the next few weeks, before he started their training again, he would let them go out to wander the fields, leave the barn open. Or, he might let them out to pasture forever. Who knew what he'd do? Would they be happy without the work? Maybe he'd take in King's snides, too, somehow. Maybe he could take care of them the way someone should. If he quit competitions, he could afford extra mouths. Such a new way of thinking.

Jeb lost, and Garnett wandered. Disbelief pushed him forward. A mournful peace hung around the field; the twilight air sang with the sounds of exiting cars in the parking lots, the rising crickets' *chip chip chipp*-ing, stragglers murmuring, and bottles trinkling into cleanup crew trash bags. It was a sad song, heavy. The whole world had settled into a new law of gravity, just for him. Where was Jeb?

And then Jaybird Olsen came up from behind, grabbed his elbow, and led him toward the parking lot.

"Garnett, your boy's done already gone."

"Oh." Garnett felt Jaybird shift his weight.

"Damn good pull, you think?"

"Not really." Garnett grimaced; he worked his blind man's wild eyes. They made people uncomfortable.

"Well, be seeing ya."

Garnett stood alone, and figured someone might offer an old man a ride. He swirled extra juices around his mouth at the smell of leftover funnel cakes. He was hungry.

The mules' bridles tinkled a tune as they walked. Jeb could've danced a jig if he didn't have the mules to hold and drive. He smiled, wide, his cheeks filling out to his ears. And then he thought about Papa. Well, the old man would have to fend for himself—he'd find somebody to help him get home. Everybody knew Papa.

Jeb avoided the route past King's snides—he'd drive Bo and Netty the long way. Tonight he'd relish freedom from everything.

Taking in a breath of tree scent and frost, Jeb looked up. The first stars blinked in the clear, cold sky. Silky stitches on an ink-colored quilt of universe and galaxy and nebulae and everything expanding and moving away and high. It smelled like snow.

It took Garnett half the night to make it out to King's property. The winter chill and bourbon hadn't helped.

Hell, he hadn't walked this property in years, but, through his filmy vision, he'd seen daybreak flame up like a match in the east and he heard the snorting, so he knew he was where he wanted. His feet ached. And his fingers had gone numb from holding the twelve-gauge in the cold air. But if King was going to neglect those mules, Garnett had to do something. His son couldn't—or wouldn't. It was all on him now. Kill those poor, miserable creatures.

In his haste, he hadn't planned on a coat or shoes. He was sure last night it would only take a few minutes; he'd scuffed on his slippers and headed right off the porch and over to the Kings'. Every lump of ground on this land had once been familiar, but he'd never ventured this far without sight and it all felt foreign now. He tripped again and again. The snowflakes fell hard and melted on his lips. Dammit, on which side of the pen were the mules standing?

A shotgun blast woke Jeb from under his warm blankets. The aluminum door and window frames of his trailer could not keep the loud burst at bay. He slipped into his boots—no socks—then pressed out into the heavy wind. Rufus lowered a cautious head and growled.

"Rufus! Boy, you stay!" Once outside, Jeb found that a rare early snow had fallen. Fine as powder, it had sieved down just enough to lend a glow to sunrise. Tree limbs over on King's property ticked against each other, an uneasy sort of twitching.

A second shot made a pop, a fast blast through the air. Jeb's head jerked to the south, to King's lower fifty where the mules corralled, where a whole flock of sparrows lifted up as a single fan, an arched smear on a newspaper-white sky. The ground crunched underfoot, but it gave a little. As he passed the stable, Bo and Netty whinnied and neighed—their trough was topped off with a web of ice. Jeb dragged his fingers through and kept going.

At the top of the rising, the wind cut through his shirt and his eyes welled up. He blinked and scanned the field—crimson snow, desperate mule. His throat thickened—below, a mule struggled, scraped on its knees, its chest slick with blood. He walked the distance. Past woods out to the road, some scrabbly, dead weeds, the gate, the mules' enclosure—its fen marshiness stiff in the cold, and Papa in his bathrobe.

Papa. Sawed-off twelve-gauge in hand, vacant eyes. Papa, all covered with dirt, blood, and straw from stumbling out there without seeing.

The old man gazed down, worked his tongue around in his mouth. He wore gaped-open pajamas, revealing his blue nakedness in the cold. On his head, little strands of mud-encrusted hair stood stiff as fence posts, even in the hard wind. He squatted down, then patted around for something at his feet, scratched at something in the snowy mud and weeds. A strange sight, as if Papa were planting seeds in the cold. Jeb sighed, quiet so as not to draw attention.

The other six unharmed mules clustered at the furthest edge of the pen, and the frozen puddle they stood upon, a mass of water left over from late fall storms, was now precarious. The poor animals' hooves had splintered right through the windowpane of ice.

And then Jeb faced the horror: the shot mule, his innards leaking from inside him, crawled by inches in a whimpering path, attempting to rejoin the pack. Jeb sighed again.

"Son, is that you? I hear you." Jeb wasn't sure if he should respond. And then Papa, still nudging at the dirt, smiled, then lifted what he'd been looking for. A shotgun shell. He loaded the gun, propped it on his hip. "Son?"

"Yes, sir."

"That bastard, King! Where's them shells?"

"You missed." Jeb pointed at the mule, though he knew Papa couldn't see a damn thing.

"Yeah, but not after this next one." Papa grinned, pinched his right eyelid shut. A laugh hissed between his lips. "I can hear that mule hard now."

"Want help?" And Jeb's voice squeaked with fear. He approached, slow.

"Boy, stand still!"

Jeb's stomach kathumped, and then he said the only thing to say.

"That mule's hit. Not square, either. You're right. It's gotta be put down—outta pain." Farm logic, encouraging, rational—it was something Papa had taught him long ago: Kill an animal fast, before it suffers.

"What you think I'm doing? King's killed 'em a long time since." Papa snorted, then blew a gob of snot from his nostril into the snow; his fogged-over eyes rolled restless.

"Hell, I can hear that mule better than I ever seen him." He lifted the gun and exhaled. The wind carried Papa's breath, a scent of bourbon, warm and rancid. Jeb smelled danger, too. Papa rambled on, muttered to himself. "Yes, sir. He killed 'em. No care to misery."

Jeb spotted a half-rotten branch, partly stobbed into the ground; he yanked it up through the frozen dirt. The icy bark numbed his hands. He waited.

And then, as if Papa meant it all along, he leveled the gun barrel at Jeb, with the rifle solid at his hip. He aimed fast.

"Or maybe I'll take you …." Papa smirked at Jeb, paused with the gun still aimed center, then shifted, pointed the barrel skyward, squeezed off an air shot, the lead fire-working in a magnificent spray. And then, as if reacting to a starting pistol, Jeb sprinted two steps forward and leapt, lunged, batted the branch at Papa's gun.

The gun went flying, smacking far off against the fence. Papa waved around, grabbed for the gun, grabbed for Jeb. He twisted, fell, and Jeb went on top of him then, his knees hard against the man's chest, his weight pushing down, and he pinned Papa's neck under the soft, dead wood of the branch. It broke in two. Papa squirmed and sat up, but Jeb grabbed him by his pajama collar and pulled him down again, thrusting a thick forearm into his throat. Papa kicked and scratched, but Jeb kept pushing. He kept pushing until he felt a little snap. With that, a mad, bubbling sound gurgled up from his windpipe.

Jeb pulled his weight off a little, but he continued to kneel on top. Papa's eyes closed now, his mouth opening and shutting as if he wanted to speak, gasping for air like a guppy out of water. He struggled; he scrapped. But Jeb knew the old man would keep trying to kill the mules. No matter how almost-dead he was. No, he would not risk it.

The two of them stayed like that for a while—Jeb bearing down, Papa flailing. Jeb, strangely, wondered if this was how men felt after reaching a mountain summit and planting a flag in the ground. The clouds above blew fast like smoke, the wind picked up. His bare ankles stung from the chill. And then there were footsteps.

"Jeb! What the hell? Heard some shots!" It was W.E. King. His voice stabbed the silence, an explosion all its own. He had his rifle, shiny and new, and he'd pulled a fur cap down over his ears.

"Go on back!" Jeb shouted, only glancing up from Papa's purple face. He maintained his hold on Papa, his forearm still pushing down. The last thing Jeb needed was King stirring things up. "Call an ambulance!"

Papa started fighting again, his energy renewed at the sound of King's voice. But Jeb held steady, held on as if life depended on this very moment. Jeb held, the cold hard now, and he pressed into Papa with effort.

It was long after King had come and gone, after so many minutes, that Papa finally went slack. Jeb turned off. Papa lay motionless; his wet head nestled in the snow. The old man's chest rose and fell in slight, labored wheezes, his breath sour and old with bourbon and his throat half-collapsed, but he was still breathing.

Jeb looked over to the pen. The wounded mule, sliding

his back legs, staggered toward the others, a slow lug and pull that had been going on since Jeb had come running.

He knew what he had to do. There was no choice. He patted the soil where Papa had been stroking it earlier, rooted around and discovered two more red shells mashed in the snow. With that, Jeb retrieved the grounded shotgun. The barrel had already turned cold; he broke it under his hands, loaded the shells, snapped the gun shut, wedged the gunstock back against the ham of his shoulder, wiped away his tears—not from the cold this time—then sighted and squeezed the trigger.

Boom. The twelve-gauge kicked, and the mule went down in slow-motion steps—to his chest, to his right shoulder, to his bloody side. Finally, in solemn surrender, the beast collapsed his thick neck to the ground and gagged in one last expiration, its ribs shuddering, then stilling, his emaciated spinal bones zagging down his back like a closed zipper. His eyes lay open, glazed in death.

At the gun's roar, the other mules had twitched and bayed. Nervous all over again, they slipped on the broken ice in the swale, looking like newborn foals with wobbly legs. Jeb dropped the gun, lifted his head. Sirens were coming round the bend, and the clouds passed slower now in the sky, filling up. He sniffed the air. The scent of danger was gone, and it smelled as if there might be more snow.

In the Yard

I go to the yard today. The yard's where the world hits you in the face—like a blast of wind when the heat won't stop. It kinda takes your breath away. The world is different here. In the yard, I'm different. Hell, I know everybody says that, but I am. And yeah, I never knew my mama, she ran off somewhere when I was a baby, but that never hurt me none. Fact is, I think it's the best thing to ever happen, truth be told. I got more'n just the sensitivities of a woman, thanks to Daddy's bringing me up. And I was fine 'til I got here with all these off-beam ladies. Shiloh Correctional Institute for Women, a flat monster of a place hugging Georgia red clay real tight. Like that kudzu they make us cut on hot summer weekends. It's hard work here, staying alive, doing the prison laundry, cleaning kitchens. But that's OK, long as I get in the yard.

I go to the yard today and think about forgiveness. I think about that time I held a knife to the lady's throat, how I needed what I needed. But it was all for nothing, now I know. If only I'd found the world wasn't so bad with me in it. That's what the Reverend Billy Witcher tells me on church Sundays and when I go in once a week. It's required that I see him. Part of the judgment. The Reverend tells me things happen for a reason. He tells me when I go to the yard, to think on it. I do. All the time. The Waffle House on Route 121 sure wouldn't have security now if I hadn't been there, the poor waitress crying about her two kids when she opened the cash register. It was only a butter knife is what I kept telling the judge.

I go to the yard today. I need to see my ants, hundreds of them. They're hardheaded babies. The way ants push that dirt around, working together, not a care in the world but living. They've got worth. They build something. Not like us ladies. We got life all torn down and scattered sideways. I think on it every day like the good Reverend tells me.

I go to the yard today, and Guard Constance J. Kiddle says, "I know you up to no good, pris'ner. Why you standing over there?" She always says that. Maybe it's true that I'm no good, but I know high quality when I see it. My ants are all about goodness. They got it together, the way they work like a team to build their mound high and move the food they find. They got purpose. Hell, I bet Noah had more than two ants on his ark.

I go to the yard today, and Guard Constance J. Kiddle sits on the bench and snores. She slumps, then snorts and sits up right quick. That dark blue suit ain't too comfortable to move in real fast, I figure. Hot, too, I bet. She frowns, her sunglasses on, arms all folded, elbows poking out like corners on a church. Them mirror lenses don't show nothing behind. Wish I had me some glasses like that.

I go to the yard today. There's action on the handball court. Some ruckus. Luella's counting cash. I rush on over.

"Hell, yeah, my bet's at two more. You wanna go higher, you pay higher," she says, taking money on something with everybody yelling back.

"No way."

"That's too much. You crazy."

I go to the yard today, and that handball court's never seen so much fuss. Most days, nobody plays nothing. Who wants to play a game when you're inside? It's already the high stakes in here. And today the stakes get higher with my red ant mound, the commotion right there on that handball court where my ants live. My heart's beating hard, like shovels digging a fast ditch.

I go to the yard today. I stand on my toes so to see over all the girls' Afros and flattops, so to see what's up. Somebody's hurting the one good thing I know—my ants. No, that's not it. They're all laughing at something else. And everybody's clapping, too. Except me. One of them bitches, Jo Beth, she's dangling a baby mouse by a string tied round its little tail, lowering it down to the ant hill so it's stung real hard, then raising it, then doing it again, again, again. She's happy to oblige the crowd, as the ants cover that baby mouse like a blanket. Luella keeps taking bets.

"Come on ladies, you can do better than that! How long will the rat take to croak?" Luella's doing a fine job running the show. That mouse, it peeps like it's crying, eyes all shut.

I go to the yard today to see my ants, but they're not fun to watch anymore. No, they're not my babies now. I push to the front and shove all my smokes at Luella, three dollars worth of tobacco; I trade a month of drags for that mouse.

"That's real nice, Miss Thing, ain't you the killer." Luella's mouth is crooked. She waits for me to continue the show, wants me to start in on the dunking.

"Damn if 1 ain't the grim reaper," I say, cupping that mouse in my hand. I take it over to the corner court so nobody can see my business. Those girls all complain and whistle, I've ruined their fun, but they get back to nothing soon enough, and I wait as they mosey on off the handball court.

I go to the yard today and I wipe him off careful. I don't pay any mind to the stings going up my arm. And then when I finish brushing off the little thing, I stomp on every last ant, grind them so hard with my boots they turn to dirt. No more ants, no more anthill.

I go to the yard today and save something. That mouse is far away by now. I'm different in the yard. Hell, I know everybody says that, but I am.

WHILE DOING MY
HAND-WASHABLES ON WEDNESDAY

I don't have a washer and dryer at my place—or a big sink, for that matter—so I go on over to Mama's, to help with her laundry and do my own. Whites on Mondays; colors, Tuesdays; and the hand-washables on Wednesdays. I just soak those in her two-sided sink for a bit, let the soap seep in real good. Well, wouldn't you know this Wednesday, that whole business, "You can't find no one," comes up with Mama. She goes on a tirade.

"Liddie, it's cuz you don't have a bosom. Your sister's always called your little ones mosquito bites, but I call 'em my great disappointment, like seeds never poppin' their heads out the dirt," Mama says, as she stands at the sink and crosses her arms, looks at my chest, and shakes her head. "You know, all the other women in the family, they all got themselves a B-cup by sixteen. And Lord knows, I thought I gave you the good genes. But your Daddy's mama was flat as a board."

Like I haven't heard all this a jillion times before. Mama goes on and on. Nothing better to talk about, I guess.

"… she was flat, all right, just like you. Now, I ask you, how you gonna settle down, marry a rich man and take care of me in my old age? How you gonna find somebody who'll take care a *you*, if there ain't no way to seduce him?" Mama's getting worked up now. "Sure you got that long, dishwater-blond hair—even if it does frizz in the heat— and you got a slim figure, but you got no chest, nothing to make those boys talk to you."

When Mama goes on like this, I get real defensive, in my mind at least; I know she'll never listen to my good plans for the future. Mama doesn't care that I want to be a paralegal and all, doesn't want to hear how it isn't important to me if I'm small-chested the rest of my born days.

My clothes are still soaking in the sink. I fold Tuesday's socks out of the dryer like pockets turned inside out, watch Mama cut biscuits into squares on the marble cutting board. Her Southern cooking would make anybody fat, but Mama doesn't care. She's got a roll around the middle and three chins. I think she's trying to get herself a heart stoppage and go on home to the Lord faster. She sure loves going to church. Gulps all the minister's words like a thirsty man needing water.

Mama's watching me as I place all my socks in the basket.

"I was wondering …," she says, "you still stuffing your bra with gym socks?"

I shake my head no, try not to push the conversation any further down the drain. She tries to be nice. She really does. But her mama was mean. That's where she gets this streak. I'm sure she loves me. Really.

"You know, you never got all that makeup and fancy stuff by me. I remember one Friday in particular when you walked past the supper table. Well, honey, I saw, plain as day, the end of a sock poking out your sleeve. Under the armpit. Your chest was all lumpy."

She's reminded me of that summer in high school. It was between sophomore and junior years, when the whole football team from Chamblee kept taking me out. I didn't give those boys any reason to think I was special, didn't let 'em see me naked, or put out, or even neck with any of them or anything like that. And I also recall that goodness: It was a trial. Oh, I stayed so pure when all I wanted was to push my crotch up real hard against the corner of a table! Truth be told, I was only good 'cuz I knew if I so much as let any of those boys do anything, they were gonna have me labeled in their locker rooms. You know how boys talk. These things cross school district lines.

"I never gave boys any reason to like me," I say, hoping Mama'll drop it.

"Well, you're never gonna find somebody at this rate, sugar," Mama says, using the sifter to sprinkle flour over the biscuit dough.

Now Mama's greasing a cookie sheet, making sure the oven's hot enough. She licks her finger and flicks the inside of the door, listening for a sizzle. It spits at her when she touches it.

"I had the boys that summer, remember, Mama?" I ask.

She looks me dead center, flour dusting her nose and cheeks. When she peers up from cooking like this, she always seems like a wide-eyed dog, startled by some siren.

"Yeah, I remember. Your bosom did look awful big, I tell you! Wonder why you couldn't hook no one for good? Did you try?"

"Well, whadya expect me to do? Give in? Lose my virginity or something?" And then I think out the rest of my answer: *Did you want me to end up like you?* I keep it to myself. Mama doesn't care about complicated things. She doesn't understand. Sure, I stuffed with socks, but I wasn't trying for any attention or anything. See, it's reverse psychology. I rolled up my white gym socks, real tight and round like eggs, then tucked them in the big nesting cups of that bra I stole out my sister's drawer. It sure was hot that summer. Especially under that nylon bra.

And mostly, I remember how I ached for *something*. Shit, those boys can make you do things. Even when you've got good resolve. And that resolve you've got when you're heading out for the evening, it just doesn't count. That "before stuff" is easy. Those nights before I went out, after I heard the doorbell chime in the hall, I remember I'd look myself in the mirror, straight in the eye, swipe on strawberry gloss, and say to myself, *No. You will say no, you will not give in. No. No. No.* But how could I say no with all those boys pushing up against me, with their fingers quivering on my waistband? It was hard, but I did it. The socks saved me. Fear of the gossip saved me. Shame saved me.

Now, Mama's humming, not noticing that I've been standing here with a pair of socks in my hands for a couple minutes. She's setting the table, putting out placemats and paper napkins. She sets a table for three.

"Mama, who's that other place for?" I ask.

"A real nice man from church, a man I like, so don't you go embarrassing me, you hear? He's a man who's right with God."

I figure this new love interest will only last a couple weeks. They always leave pretty fast with Mama. All my life, she's tried not to show her needs. She does pretty good at pushing things away. It's the mean streak, I figure.

"Liddie, now stop your sulking and start rinsing those clothes out. I need to get in that sink."

I run cold water over the clothes, and when it runs clear, I mash on my good lavender blouse, sure not to wring—that's what the tag instructs. I think as I twist my double-A bras until they're not even dripping that it's good I don't have a bosom. Yeah, who wants a man? They all puff up with promises they never keep, anyway. That's what's happened to Mama. They promise and then they leave. Like clockwork.

I throw my damp clothes in a net bag, put them aside to hang later. The doorbell rings and Mama unties her apron real fast, flings it on top of the refrigerator, smooths her stray hairs, and bolts for the door. When she comes back, she has hold of this man's elbow and she's smiling. Wide. She has a pink flush to her face that makes her almost pretty; her oxford shirt's frayed at the cuffs, but otherwise she looks good. Mama's new man's wearing a pressed khaki suit and white buck shoes. Pretty fancy stuff for this house.

"Liddie, I'd like you to meet the Honorable Mr. Wiley Jay Oates. Mr. Oates, my daughter, Liddie."

"Nice to meet such a lovely daughter," he smiles and raises his eyebrows, pushes his hand out for me to shake. I could swear he's leering at me with his one brown eye, one blue. The blue eye chases something around in its socket. I shake his hand and he smiles. His greased-down hair makes his nose poke out like a beak or something, and his brow is beading up with sweat.

"Your hands clean?" Mama asks no one in particular and washes her own for about the thirtieth time, then sits down.

"No, ma'am!" Mr. Oates chuckles and we both run our hands under the faucet. He brushes up a little too close for my comfort. I pretend not to notice. But then, when he presses his leg into my hip, I reach over the sink for a towel to dry my hands and dribble water on his nice suede shoes. His Adam's apple bobs up and down, like a pulse, as he clears his throat.

Mama speaks up. "Come on, you two; it's gonna get cold." She's sitting at the end of the table and bows her head. We all grasp hands for prayer, tilt our heads down, and Mama whispers her thanks. As I hold Mr. Oates' hand, he wiggles his finger in my palm. I just listen to Mama, the steam rising from those biscuits in the bread basket, and I wait for her to finish so I can cut a big one open and slather a big glob of melting margarine all inside it.

As she finishes her prayer, "And let Liddie here, Lord, find a man. We need it. Amen," I look up and Mr. Oates hits a wink at me with his good, brown eye. I pass Mama the biscuit basket.

Look, I want to say, I can get mine all by myself—money and pleasure, thank you very much. I also want to remind Mama I'm going to be a paralegal, that I'm going to do the mail correspondence course you see on the TV, that I'm going to get rich all by myself. No man needed. Hell, I know that love stuff's not real. I know men prop you up with promises and then they disappear. Just like what'll happen with the Honorable Mr. Wiley Jay Oates' affection for Mama.

And, man, I want to tell her, too, that I'm glad I had my insurance policy in those socks that summer! I still have a good reputation. Well, more like no reputation. But here and now, who needs any kind of reputation, good or bad? Don't need no one or nothing. Yeah, I want to say all this stuff to Mama and Mr. Oates, but I don't. I just watch Mama attack her food, chewing on both sides of her mouth. Mr. Oates licks his lips and flashes his eye at me again. I get up and go outside to hang my delicates on the line.

Next week, supper will be different. Sure, I'll still be washing my whites come Monday, my colors on Tuesday, but I guarantee that Mama and I'll be sitting down to a table set for two, not three, after I do the hand-washables on Wednesday, after all the grime circles on down the drain.

Beware the Moon

The wolves came to her tent late that night. And she was not afraid, though that was not really unusual.

Earlier, summer twilight arrived with creaking grasshoppers and crickets. Then the larger animals joined their song, heaving in the dusky shadow woods behind her. The bigger creatures snarled and licked, waiting for their moment, as they had every night she had camped here. No one was around, not for miles. And she liked it that way. Her guitar was enough. It kept her company, made her safe. Her clear voice accompanied the twangs and strums of her twelve-string, trailing above the woods; she sang woeful and pure, the funny words of a nineteen-year-old. The pack of wolves up the hill joined in as they had the night before—their key matched her own yodeling breaths. They were one.

She leaned over to stoke embers in the fire, then gazed to the heights. The night sky above the mountains dwindled with lavender cream streaks; deep lapis blue soon melted into purple, and then, finally, a slow unraveling of stars spilled out of the thick blanket sky. She'd hoped for a full moon this last night in the wilderness. She'd gotten one. And so she sang and picked until the fire was almost out, then scrambled into her tent to fall into a deep sleep.

A noise, a sound, something outside. She woke in fuzziness, not sure how long she'd been dreaming, but sure there was something outside, sure she now heard sniffing or scratching or something that was not the wind. It was still dark, she knew this much, though with the moon she did not need her flashlight. She squinted, looked around in the bluish, underwater glow inside her tent: Her dark-adapted eye found everything: deep cherry guitar, red sleeping bag, blue parka. She lay awake. Still, no fear. There never was any fear, really, so this solitary trip began as a test. She hoped for something, to squeeze "true life and emotion" out of her songs—something the music critics said she lacked.

They had faulted her stoicism in their reviews.

It was true: She was never sure if she'd had real feelings. About anything. Certainly, when she worked on chords late into the night or vibrato notes low on the neck of her guitar for hours at a stretch, writing songs about things she could not understand, her fingers would bleed and sting. Physical pain was one thing, but she'd never truly experienced a depth of emotions that she noticed in others. Tears for good-byes, tears for births, tears at weddings and funerals. She witnessed these times with her friends and family, sat through ceremonies, and somehow in the midst of others' pains and joys, her body was not hers. She would float above herself in the cold Canadian days, the summers and winters, and see everyone and everything as if it all were fluttering by in a snow globe or in a sepia-toned movie, herself peering in, blank-faced and pale. Only when she was on stage, singing in a small, candlelight performance hall did she feel any semblance of love for people.

Now, above her groggy head in the tent, she could make out patterns. The trees silhouetted in the wind, crocheting branches of black lace, twining in angry pointed images, moving, alive. Her breath was foggy in the cold June night.

Again, there was the same scratching and scraping in the thin air that had awoken her. And there was something new: an angry whining, a snarling. The raspy respirations were louder now. She slumped under her sleeping bag, kicked it around.

A loud bay. A shockwave. The tent trembled.

And then, a terrible slashing sound jolted her completely awake. She felt cold wind whistle at her neck. The full moon's face smirked down on her through a rip in her tent. She closed her eyes to its accusations, and there were prickly footsteps stalking all around her, sniffing, and the rancid, dark, metallic scent of a meat-eater's breath ruffled her hair.

Her guitar was just in reach; it glistened in the eerie light, and when she grabbed at it, the instrument thudded and gave out a sharp yelp, strings scraping dissonance against the ground. Teeth ripped at her then; there was a hard pain in her shoulder, and she was tugged out under the sky, the stars and moon mocking floodlights, the woods far off. She clutched for something to hold onto, anything. Dry grass and loam. Nothing. She tried to cry out, but her throat was caught by something sharp. The only noise she could make was a rasping gurgle. Everything spun around her; her ears filled with a roaring, and the teeth came, again and again, tugging, tugging, devouring, and warm blood, her own, so much blood. And there was feeling; it gushed. They were one.

SKIMMING STONES

A murmuration of starlings took wing in the cemetery, dimmed a mohair blue sky, its cabinet of clouds. Flashes of birds' tails and beaks reflected in my black patent pumps, and I knew, in that moment, that I was experiencing what they call dry grief. Grandmother Ann was dead. No crying. No wailing. Just a stone, heavy, that couldn't climb the hill of my heart. I was comfortable in that yawning place. It was familiar.

Whee, wheeeee, the circling birds called, like kids having fun, thousands of songs ghosting in the breeze. A skin of summer light, just enough for heat, settled around me. And the shiny coffin lowered on its straps. I tried to take my cousin Larkin's hand, my adult cousin, who was dressed in her superhero garb—cape and all—but she pushed my hand away. That morning, before the lonely service, I'd let her dress for the funeral as her alter ego, a made-up comic book champion named Danger Blade. I allowed her to go everywhere like that; after all, Grandmother Ann would not have cared, and, thank God, Larkin's costume kept her calm, kept her quiet.

We were the sole attendees at the burial, the only people in the graveyard, the only people left of Grandmother's kith and kin—all her relatives and friends were gone; they'd passed years before I even came along. Yes, Larkin and I stood alone among tombstones lined up along their rows like good soldiers. We were good soldiers, too. The gravediggers finished up; they threw shovelfuls of dirt into the grave, and the sound of dry clay slapped the coffin below. I turned away, went to the parking lot. With no words between us, Larkin, my cousin—Danger Blade—followed me at a distance until we were in my car.

Next to me in the front seat, Larkin hummed something that sounded like the theme song from *Spider-Man—Spins a web, duh-duh-duh, watch out! Duh-duh-da-duh-duh ....* I couldn't help but think, as I glanced at her, with her feet up on the dash, that she was returning home to the only bed she'd ever slept in. And now the house would be sold. Larkin was mine now. Just like the grief. But I made jokes, tried to put her at ease. It wasn't a snap, for sure. Her level of understanding was basic. Or maybe she heard me in a different way.

We crossed town in just a few minutes, headed for Maple Street. I tried the joke about the priest, then the one about the one-legged man. Larkin did not break a smile.

"You know, Audrey," Larkin interrupted, "Daddy laughed himself to death." Funny, she was right. Her father, my Uncle Kenny, a happy man with bad eating habits, had a heart attack one night at the local comedy showcase. According to witnesses at the time, he'd been laughing so hard he'd fallen off his chair. No one ever saw the big man lapse into heart trouble.

I veered off Main and thought about my other autistic cousin, thirty-three-year-old Willie, Larkin's younger brother. He was home with a sitter. Because both Larkin and Willie were autistic, I promised Grandmother Ann I'd take care of them. No homes, no separation. I'd gotten two kids of my own, adults with the minds of children. It could've been worse, but not much.

I thought about Grandmother Ann, the day I'd promised her. It was in the hospital, as her end drew near, and the old woman looked fragile as a doll, arms and legs stiff as she lay in her bed with all its cranks and hoses. The sickness made it easier, I assumed, for the old woman to express her real opinions.

"You gotta watch 'em, Audrey. Promise me, y'all have to stay together. You're my only family. My only …," Grandmother Ann hissed her demand in a half-whisper, tugging at her nasal tubing as she leaned in toward me. She wanted to make sure Larkin didn't hear; my cousin was outside the door in the waiting room, watching a talk show on TV.

"Kick his butt, lady! He done you wrong!" Larkin hollered, and then she was up and jogging down the hall past Grandmother Ann's open door, her cape buffeting behind her like a dark cloud. Grandmother's hand, slippery from lotion, clenched my own. It was an unspoken signal. The oxygen machine wheezed, *Ppppsssssssssss!* as the old lady's chest rose and fell in bursts. She fell asleep, reassured that I would take care of everything. Damn.

It hit me on the drive home from the funeral. How the hell was I supposed to look after my cousins? I couldn't even look after myself.

A big cross with the words "Jesus Saves" blinked its message over the intersection as Larkin and I passed through, the blue neon pointless in broad daylight. I turned off Maple and into the town park where, from the road, I saw ducks circling a placid pond.

"Why don't we stop here for a little bit?" I said, cutting off the engine and kicking off my shoes. Larkin pulled off her boots and thigh-high tights, her pale legs furry, part of her bare behind bulging as her purple leotard rode up her left butt cheek. We walked through the stubby grass, hopping over the spots with sharp gravel. At the muddy edge of the pond, with oozy red clay cooling our toes, Larkin and I started skimming stones; we did it at the same time, as if the idea was there all along just waiting for us. The ducks hurried their swim and dodged our missiles, then waddled to shore on the other side, avoiding our tossed rocks all the while. On the bank, they clucked at us, stomping the ground with their webbed feet.

I couldn't stop thinking about Grandmother Ann. She was gone, and, for me, there was nothing left of her but scant memories. And, of course, I had my guardian duties, something I did not want. Love was not even part of the picture.

"Hey, Audrey, you know what? Love makes people real," Larkin said, jutting her chin out. "Just like the Velveteen Rabbit."

She could've been reading my mind. Her eyes, so wide you could see shadows and light sparking in the irises, were moist behind her thick, heavy-framed glasses. She overhanded a smooth stone far across the pond, barely missed a mother duck and her two young ones nestled on the opposite bank. At that moment, I felt nothing but that hard spot in my heart and wished I could cry, too. It was obvious that Larkin understood Grandmother Ann was gone for good; she somehow knew it in her own way. I rubbed a smooth, warm pebble in my fingers, pitched it hard. It bounced five times, then plunked below on its last, short jump.

We skipped stones in silence like that a little longer, then headed home. In moments, we pulled up in the driveway, and I heard Larkin swallow hard. Cousin Willie came barreling out the ranch-style house yelling how he wanted an "... orange rain slicker ... with a floppy hat and a string for under the chin, and a real metal clasp and matching galoshes and gloves, Paddington Bear, Paddington Bear, the bear at Paddington." His suspenders, with bright pink pigs stamped on them, were a little crooked, but his eyes were adamant behind his own thick glasses. Good eyes were never part of the Perloff gene pool. My own astigmatism attested to that.

Miss Ora Lee, Willie's occasional sitter from down the street, a lady who Larkin trusted, tapped on my windshield. I squeaked down my window.

"He's been goin' on all day about that bear," she said, arms crossed. "Bet the funeral was nice. Wish I coulda been there." Without waiting for me to respond, she continued, "Guess I'll be heading on home now, if you don't mind. Got supper to fix."

"Thanks. You really saved the day," I said and grabbed my wallet. I pulled out a twenty and a five and handed them over.

"You be good, Willie," Miss Ora Lee said. He ignored her, as he bellowed his refrain, "The bear at Paddington, Paddington Bear, Paddington Bear." She shook her head and smiled at me, as if she felt sorry for all of us.

"I'll be praying for your grandmother and *all*," she said, emphasizing "all," and wobbled on down the street, her hair the color of a bright pink Easter egg. She folded her money as she went.

So Larkin and I sat in the car a while. I hesitated, not sure what to do next. She found some nail polish in my purse, which she opened. The polish dribbled down her leg, "Like blood," she giggled as she proceeded to paint her toenails. Willie prowled the yard, then settled on the car, pressed his face to each window, stared at us as if we were animals in a cage at the zoo. He discovered the back door was open. Once inside, he decided on rummaging through the contents of my backseat, which contained all my earthly possessions.

☾

I'd arrived at Grandmother Ann's in a hurry when she took a bad turn and ended up in the hospital. I left a job, a boyfriend, and an apartment in Boston for Warm Springs. For this. My secretarial job for an import/export wasn't that fulfilling anyway, and Gary, my boyfriend, was already on his way out—commitment issues (his, not mine). Hell, I guess I was dealing with some issues, too—I didn't even want a goldfish. All I ever needed were some clothes, my car, and the tool chest I'd been toting since California.

California's where I went after Mom and Dad died. They died when I was a kid. By the time I was grown, my parents had become only out-of-focus memories. Every so often, I still felt something sharp when I thought of them. In the recesses of my mind, there were faint reminiscences embossed there—a slight whisper of perfume, sitting on a feather bed somewhere, a dry kiss on the cheek. And, really, I'm not so sure if those memories were of my parents, or if those things even happened. Maybe I saw them in a movie.

But Dad's mother, my grandmother, Nana Beth, felt her duty to reassure me often of my parents' feelings for me. She told me they loved me "terrible" before they were hit by "that damned eighteen-wheeler" on the highway. Yes, it was after their funeral when Nana Beth took me in. "Promise me, ya hear, you'll always know they cared? They really did."

For most of my childhood, Nana Beth and I lived in California in an apartment building. Nana Beth was a widow—I never heard any mention of my grandfather,

her husband. Not even a photo. I was curious about my grandfather, but she never gave me any information about the man. I figured he hadn't been too nice.

Nana Beth was a slight, strong woman in her fifties who introduced herself to strangers, "Hello, so nice to meet you. I'm Elizabeth Painter, the church sexton on leave." Later, in high school, I looked up sexton in the dictionary: "A church maintenance custodian." I guess that would explain why Nana Beth's rickety station wagon was weighed down with every tool in existence. She was funny, strange in a good way, and she stuttered, especially in the mornings or after naps, as if her mouth took a while to wake up. "Mmmm-mmmorning."

I remember Nana Beth always doing the opposite of every other parent or guardian: Before breakfast, she'd buy me candy bars and sweets at the gas station; on weekdays, when I should've been in school, she'd take me to the park; and in the middle of a heat wave, she'd pull hot biscuits and Christmas cake from the oven. Nana Beth was more than a grandmother; she was my best friend. And, as I got older, in high school, I'd sit up nights with her, eat peanuts, and watch the late-late show and talk about boys. We were a strange family. But we were a family.

And then she was gone and I had no one. Within a month of my going off to college, Nana Beth was dead. The massive coronary hit fast, and she passed away in the ambulance before she even got to the hospital. I received the phone call after the fact. I didn't cry then, either. Not even when I went home for the funeral and packed up her stuff and the apartment. Her toolbox was still sitting in my trunk as I sat there with my cousins in Warm Springs.

Larkin and I listened to Willie count all the stitches in the vinyl back seat, tapping his fingers on the window with each number "One forty-one, one forty-two, one forty-three ...." Grandmother Ann must have meant as much, if not more, for Larkin and Willie as Nana Beth had meant to me. And now Grandmother Ann was gone, too.

It was after Nana Beth died that I reacquainted myself with Grandmother Ann, Mom's mother, and these two cousins. Mom's family was from the South, a place I'd only heard and read about—Warm Springs. A mythic-sounding place, so many beautiful images in the name. Warm. Springs. In college, after Grandmother Ann found out I was all alone, she kept close contact—no letters or visits, just phone calls. Lots of them. She called me up with the latest news, in need of an ear; she always said she needed to talk to "someone who's family." Sometimes she called at two a.m., breathless, with the latest trouble, asking for advice. It was always about my cousins. For a while there, it was one tough break after another for my oldest cousin, Larkin. And Grandmother Ann could not control her.

Grandmother Ann once told me that Larkin possessed a milder variant of autistic disorder, Asperger's syndrome. When I finally came here to meet her, Larkin fit the psychological profiles I'd read. (I wanted to meet my family prepared, so I studied everything I could find on autism.) Because she was high-functioning, Larkin was "with it" enough to know she wasn't "with it." And my cousin keenly felt her disadvantage. I saw her self-consciousness, watched her when strangers approached; her shoulders would slump and she wouldn't meet anyone's eyes. She showed her awareness, too, in the way she protected her brother from outsiders. He was worse off and she knew it. So far, she had not allowed me to talk to Willie without her around; she flanked me whenever I came too close to him.

In my readings, I discovered that those with Asperger's usually chose a circumscribed area of interest that left no space for age-appropriate, common interests. People with Asperger's could obsess over cars, trains, French literature, doorknobs, hinges, cappuccino, meteorology, astronomy, history, or whatever. But, fortunately, for Larkin, she fixated on something positive, something she could use to deal with the world. To a certain extent, at least. Yes, she devised an alter ego, metamorphosed herself into a superhero, a real, honest-to-goodness caped crusader—Danger Blade. Over the years, she accumulated the costume: plush purple tights and leotard, midnight blue tunic and black cape, and a belt pushed crotchward by her round belly.

Whenever Larkin felt threatened, she became Danger Blade, would slip into her outfit and cover her glasses with a silver-sequined mask she wore imperiously upon her head. I figured that Larkin's superhero was the end product of all the events and interests of her past— rejections and sexual predators and comic books and wrestling. Everything that ever happened to Larkin compounded in her autistic mind. Danger Blade was as real now as Larkin.

So, I sat there on that hot summer day with my two cousins in the car in the driveway, the day we buried Grandmother Ann, the thick smell of nail polish nauseating as Larkin continued to paint her nails a bright crimson. I wasn't sure what to do with these two. I remembered Grandmother Ann's own inability to control them. There was that call from Grandmother Ann, crying over the phone lines, telling me, "The girl hasn't eaten a bite for a week." Another time Grandmother Ann called, sniffling about Larkin's assault. "Audrey, the girl walked up to the Winn Dixie half-cocked and met some con man who talked her into taking her clothes off in the back room. Thank God they got cameras in those places and someone found them in time …." And as I sat there and picked at my peeling dashboard, I decided to ask Larkin some personal things.

"Who's Danger Blade exactly?" She harrumphed, as she dripped nail polish on her knuckles.

"She's a mutant superhero raised by chickens. She's got instant language understanding; she can manipulate energy and she's strong. She don't like men who prey on the helpless. And she can use this here necklace to ward off any evil." With a wet nail, Larkin plucked at the chain, the pendant a silver chicken claw grasping a crystal ball. "Danger Blade may be disabled, but she can do things no one else can. She's a defender!" She jabbed the necklace in the air like a dagger. Willie opened the back door and scooted out with my old backpack.

"It's hot, hot, hot, and I want a raincoat, a rubber raincoat."

"And Larkin, what does *Larkin* do?" I asked, ignoring Willie's rant, wanting a better answer from Larkin, something concrete.

"The worst things ever," Larkin said matter-of-factly as we watched Willie pace the driveway. "I had a fake wedding. When I was in the hospital for evaluations, they drugged me up on something. It made me stupid. And then I got hitched. Not a real wedding at all, no white dress, no flowers, just some old man reading from the Bible …. Oh, I'm still so embarrassed!" She covered her mouth, her eyes wide and her face turned the color of Miss Ora Lee's hair.

"I didn't need those drugs, they made me do crazy things. Grandma Ann had it annulled. That stupid guy, well, we didn't have any sex, if you're wondering. Yuck. You know, my ex-husband rode the short bus." We both giggled.

"You're a long-bus gal, Larkin," I said. She brightened and spoke with conviction.

"You know, Danger Blade don't need a man, anyway. She's disabled, but kicks ass." She pumped her fist, her admiration of Danger Blade making her voice quiver. I was beginning to see that in Larkin's life, Danger Blade was more real than anything. Yes, Larkin spoke of her super hero alter ego in the third person. With reverence. Whereas, her own name, when she said it, was pushed out between clenched teeth as if it were a bad word.

Grandmother Ann's opinion of Danger Blade had not been generous; she confided in me often those last days at the hospital, the oxygen machine wheezing for her, "If only I could get her to quit all that Danger Blade stuff. I think it's her way of coping with what that man did to her up at the Winn-Dixie, though. You be careful when she's like that, you hear? She's a loose cannon. It all just gives me the heebie-jeebies. The girl needs a job."

Now, Larkin wouldn't want for anything, job or no job. With Grandmother Ann gone, the sale of the old lady's house and her savings, along with the disability assistance they already received from the state, would keep Larkin and Willie comfortable for the whole of their lives.

Willie slid into the car again, lowered and raised the back windows, spun the handles with furious speed. I let him fiddle for a few minutes until the heat and the sharp scent of nail polish got to me, and then I made a pronouncement.

"Come on, guys. We're gonna get something to drink," I said, the lines of sweat trickling down from the creases behind my knees. I got out and slammed the car door, hoping they'd follow. They did. One step at a time. That's all it would take with these two.

On the porch, we stopped so Danger Blade could profess her mission. Ever since I'd arrived, it was the same routine. The porch, the entry or exit to the outside world, set Larkin off every time, whether we were heading to the mailbox or the shopping mall or coming home from wherever.

"Danger Blade will rid this country of evil. She's going global, I tell you!" As she yelled this to no one in particular, she advanced her right foot forward in a quasi-calisthenic stretch, extended her left arm, and clenched her fist. In answer to Danger Blade's plaintive cry, there was only a wave of cicadas humming, the sound moving in and out, loud, then silent. I smiled, Willie tugged at Larkin's hand, pulling at her. This was all very uncomfortable. The three of us stood there a moment on the porch of Grandmother Ann's house, which was set back from the quiet road. We surveyed the corner property, the big oaks in the yard like shading sentinels. Down the hill, out in the sun, the asphalt cooked in the late summer heat.

We walked inside, headed for the kitchen, and I asked, "You guys want some lemonade or something?" Not waiting for an answer, I grabbed the jug from the fridge, and they tagged along behind me back to the swings on the porch. I felt like the Pied Piper.

Later that week, with the house on the market, the FOR SALE sign poking in the yard at the curb, we started cleaning. I decided we'd sort and donate Grandmother Ann's stuff. For hours, we pulled all kinds of things from Grandmother's bureaus and closets and piled them onto the bed. I directed Willie and Larkin to fold the clothes. We filled more than two dozen boxes with flowered muumuus and caftans and scarves and gold and silver and beige sandals. Willie mainly watched and walked laps through the house.

"Hey, Audrey, you think this'll make a good belt for Danger Blade? You think she'll like it?" Larkin held up a long, sapphire blue length of suede.

"Sure, what the hey; it's a great color for a superhero." I tried to sound as enthusiastic as I could. Larkin tied it around her waist and smiled into the mirror.

I was lost in family memories I'd never had. I'd never see Grandmother Ann wear the green leisure suit I held up to the overhead light, with its big, red stain on the chest. It looked like ketchup or hot sauce, maybe something from a barbecue. I tossed it in the trash. I thought about all the family events I'd missed over the years. No, I'd never celebrate any holidays or birthdays with a now-dead grandmother I never got to know. Now I felt the pressure of time. I was supposed to make this situation with my cousins work.

"No raincoats, no rubber raincoats, no Paddington Bear, Bear, Bear," Willie repeated his chorus as he jumped on the bed. The Goodwill boxes bounced as he bounded up and down. Oh God, could I make this work all day, every day?

"I'll be right back, guys." I went to call Goodwill from the kitchen phone and left Larkin, looking in the mirror, clipping on some dangle earrings that looked like chandeliers. Willie was still jumping on the bed.

Dusted in old crumbs, the Formica table in the breakfast nook was as I left it from breakfast, though I imagined it had never been wiped clean; the wallpaper was yellowed with age, the ashtray on the counter still piled high with Grandmother Ann's butts from weeks ago. Underneath the table were stacks two feet high of romance novels. On the book covers, swarthy pirates clutched swooning, breasty wenches. The whole place reminded me of a

Seventies sitcom. It was as if time stood still after Uncle Kenny had his heart attack.

I turned—Larkin was standing in the doorway, poised to pounce. I smiled. She did not smile back. No, she'd been watching me awhile as I'd waited with the receiver tucked between my ear and shoulder. I was on hold. Goodwill had me on hold.

"You giving all her clothes away? You can't do that. Danger Blade won't let you." She moved closer, fast and sideways like a cat, and then she was on me and I couldn't respond or make a noise as she pulled me into a head-lock. She growled, she laughed, I was looking at one of Grandmother Ann's earrings pinching her earlobe, turn-ing it a bright red, the shade, I imagined, of my own face as I gasped for air.

"I've seen 'em do this halfnelson on Worldwide Wrestling. They do it all the time!" An edge, an angry tone, crept into her sweet voice, and she gripped my neck tight, and her grasp tightened even more, and I swooned like the women on all the romance novel covers spread across the floor. As I fell, as I moved down into unconsciousness, I grabbed at Larkin's bright tights, snagging a long run up her calf, and, at the end of my fall, as I lay on the floor, I gazed at Larkin's fat big toe, which poked through a hole in her tights, and everything in my eyes darkened and finally went to nothing.

That was the last I saw of Larkin, really, for a while. After the ambulance came (I assumed she knew how to call

9-1-1), and I was in the emergency room with a collapsed trachea and broken collarbone, they carted my cousins over to the state hospital at Milledgeville. They'd transfer out at some point in the next week.

It was a bright day outside, a high, yellow sun and a clear sky. The dew in the grass shivered like drops of mercury, and a lonely hawk looped in low thermals above the street. I could see the whole world, it felt, from that bay window. In the dark, empty throat of the foyer, I found Danger Blade's cape and chicken claw necklace flung like afterthoughts on the coat tree. Larkin must have left them there before the ambulance scurried her away. So much for ridding the world of evil.

I was back at the house, liquidating the estate, with a stiff therapeutic collar cuffing my neck. It was slow going and I still hurt from the top of my head on down. Couldn't lift much. I pointed out things to the movers; they took orders. The house had brought a pretty penny. Quick, too. There was enough, combined with Grandmother Ann's savings, for the exorbitant care (and costs) Larkin and Willie would require—I'd arranged for one of those private daycare centers for them both during the weekdays. As for living arrangements, I bought a condominium half a mile away from their program where I could take charge of them at night. At least the three of us wouldn't be separated all the time. The counselors said I needed to think about my safety. At least Larkin would have supervision during the day.

I slipped on the silver mask Larkin had left forgotten on the hall table, and, in the entrance mirror, I saw my own graven reflection staring back at me. The distance between my pain and my heart narrowed. Tears welled up. They'd been a long time coming. That stone below my chest was finally shifting, not lifting so much, but raising a little to let the feelings trickle on in. It all came clear. The days before me sprang up from a deep well; the years on the calendar would collect in snags of commotion, a force I would try to control. I would shed my comfort of deadness. Yes, I would imitate my cousin's superhero resolve. I would stay. There was no leaving. My promise to Grandmother Ann was one I meant to keep.

Come to Me

My five-year-old cousin, Caleb, hobbles from a line of tall weeds, all thinned out along the clay road. There's a limp in his step. *Come to me, little cousin; I see you crying.*

I sit in the grass and wait for him. All afternoon, I've whiled away the hours, pulling pokeweeds, splitting the stalks with green-stained fingers, swirling the vinegary taste of the plant with my tongue, imagining a pretend family.

Here comes Caleb, his walk sideways with some kind of hurt. When he gets near me, he cries louder. Grateful, relieved. He sits beside me in the crushed-down weeds, scuffs off both his corrective shoes, and holds up his right foot. He must wear his thick-soled shoes every day, but he keeps them untied, the tongues and laces loping over his exposed soft baby skin.

"I got a bite out there, Willa," he says and points to the dim woods, no sunlight inside. "A snake. I got a snake bite." Caleb smells like play, his hair full of summer sweat and dark things, too. The ankle is red, and the blood dots trickle bright. I kneel down and hold his foot in my hand.

I command, "Sit still!" I don't like how the bite is looking, his foot puffing all around. Blue jays argue, wrestle in the willow trees along the path. They debate the bite, all the threats in the world. The sun is behind the house now, but the top of Caleb's head still shines with heat. I'm hot, too. I go down on my knees and put my mouth to Caleb's heel, suck at the small punctures. There is the taste of blood and tin in the venom. I draw more and spit it into the grass. Caleb is quiet, concentrating.

"Is it gonna kill me, Will?"

"I don't know. It might."

Everything's Lighter
in Water

The lake was choppy, *Angry with fish*, Grandpa had said. And Tara, who was skipping junior high for the third time that week, wormed a good hook for him, used one of those purple plastic worms Grandpa got mail order. They stood shoulder to shoulder on the weather-beaten dock, the vast, depthless brown of water and the world beyond. The buzz of an outboard off in the distance broke the silence every so often. And above, the sun glared down and blinked, as if the billowing, mounting rain clouds were eyelids. The water was a pulse, like a heartbeat, and underneath Tara knew there were flashing shoals of fish, forests of green fungus and weeds.

Grandpa and Tara stood silent, spinning rods in hand, lures and purple worms sizzling out over the water, breaking the surface once in a while. They waited for a twitch on the line, for weather, for something. As it turned out, the day on the dock unfolded into a long one—there were problems. There always were. The clouds filled and emptied, and, in flashes of lightning, the pine trees skewered the banks like darts. The murky lake swelled over the high -water mark.

"We gotta get inside, for safety's sake," Grandpa hollered as they hoofed it up the hill through the torrents. By the time they ducked under the porch eave, Grandpa was wheezing louder than the slapping rain. They waited until the thunder passed.

"Grandpa, you think the fish knew the storm was coming?"

"That's a good way of looking at it. Never used that excuse before. Buddies down at the Rotary'll like that one," Grandpa chuckled, tousled her hair. She could see the deep creases around his eyes crinkle. "I do know those fish'll like all the bugs and worms come out from the storm now," he said. So, at last, when slices of sun filtered through the drizzle, they began fishing again. The world smelled clean then, the pine and the rotting leaves on the hill giving off a sweet scent.

But the fish waited to nibble until late.

"Guess our theory wasn't so right," Grandpa said. It was Grandpa who had no luck at all, and Tara's first fish broke her line. But by midafternoon, Tara hooked, then reeled in, with a few jerks and a quick pull, a fine catch. About a four-pounder.

"You didn't think we'd get anything today, did you Grandpa?"

"Not too shabby. Kid, you done good. Guess being thirteen's not too unlucky." His creases crinkled again. Tara smiled, too, her freckly cheeks all warm in the sun. She was happy she'd pleased him. The fish she'd caught was long and brown, not very pretty, not a rainbow trout by any means. Its eyes bulged at Tara from the metal tub. She named him Floyd. She always gave her catches "F" names.

They kept on fishing. All kinds of bullfrogs and little toads came out. They *barumphed* and whistled their sad songs all day; they sang whenever the sun rolled like a big ball behind the clouds. Grandpa told Tara, "Thirty-one types of frogs and toads live all over this state, dontcha know? All those sounds they make? They're love calls. Think of it, Tara, those frogs looking for somebody just like the rest of us."

It was four-thirty on the dot (Grandpa's watch was always right), when Ruth, Tara's stepmother, skidded to a stop up at the house; they could hear gravel spraying, pelting all the wooden posts on the porch.

"There's always hell to pay," Grandpa mumbled as he balanced the base of his pole next to the tackle box. His line, still out, stayed taut, and the silver gleam of his propped rod slit the air like a sardonic smile. Grandpa stood there, waiting. Tara heard a car door slam, and, then, like a surfer, David, her stepbrother, coasted in his high tops down the hill, slid to the dock on a carpet of waxy pine straw in two long, skidding trails. Tara pretended not to notice, as she bent over the galvanized tub where Floyd, her catch, churned and wiggled in his water. Out of the corner of her eye, she saw David shake Grandpa's hand, saw him spy Floyd over Grandpa's shoulder. She tried not to stare. Her fish swirled around in his tub, oblivious to his frying pan fate, and David peered over.

"Cool. A girl who can actually catch something."

"She's more'n that," Grandpa volunteered, patting Tara on the back, smiling so wide she could see his pink gums. David blinked at Tara, combed back his bangs with long, tawny fingers, revealed his poker-straight lashes, and she felt that flip in her stomach. He was much taller than she remembered.

"I'll have a go," David said, and Tara handed him a pole. In silence, they wormed and lured their hooks. Grandpa yawned, folded into his lawn chair on the muddy bank, then shined a green apple, sawed it back and forth across his chest. It squeaked like a rusty hinge as he rubbed it clumsily against his rough denim shirt. His right thumb, wrapped in a wad of dirty gauze, wasn't making the job too easy.

Injuries were normal for Grandpa. Since she'd moved up here, he'd hurt himself so many times she'd quit counting. They stocked an inventory of Band-Aids and antiseptic and dressings in the medicine cabinet. "Enough for the Third Army," Grandpa always said. She wondered if he'd been like this when Grandma was alive. Every day it was something else. He'd come out of his workshop or garden cussing, blood on some body part: "Goddamned screw! Shit shovel! You'd think .... Damn those people .... Don't know how to make nothing."

Tara knew the drill. So many times, she'd stifle her grin, pretend she hadn't heard his profanities; she even tried to help out. Just yesterday, he'd hurt that thumb in some accident with a hammer, and he couldn't handle anything with much of a grip. Tara watched him struggle all last night as he fumbled with everything—tools, candles, forks, fruit—and watched him now as he was clumsy with the apple in his bad hand, as he grunted and chewed slow.

Hey, missy, that's why I need your help today. Need you to hook my bait and maybe cast, too. Damn thumb … but we need dinner, you know …, he'd told her that this morning. It was after Ruth called at nine a.m., sharp. Tara knew what he was really doing, why they were fishing. In the rain even. There was food enough in the freezer. She smiled; Grandpa smiled back through his last bite and scudded the skinny apple core into the lake with his good hand. It floated up and down like the red and white bobbers they used sometimes.

"Hey, David, guess your mother's probably up there snooping, you think?" Grandpa asked.

"You know it," David said.

"Guess I'll let her. No harm. She can't do nothing." And as Grandpa settled in for a snooze, she saw him relax for the first time all day. He propped his elbow on his knee, his gauze-wrapped thumb like a mummy.

So David and Tara fished. Tossing his line out, David inhaled. The lure sailed a distance with a hiss, then landed, marring the mirrored surface of water with a ripple. He exhaled smoothly just as the lure hit with a splat. Tara's line followed, fell far short, and plunked down, loud, announcing her failed attempt. She reeled in, recast. It skimmed the surface. David smiled.

"Hey, don't scare off my fish," he said. There was silence again. At least for a few minutes. "By the way, I hear you're skipping school. Watch Mom; she's pissed." He kept his eye trained on the lake and tossed his line out again, this time farther, where the big fish lurked, in the shadowy, deep arena of water weeds.

"Thanks for the heads-up." Yeah, Tara knew Ruth was pissed. Why else would she be there? She handled her reel and gazed at Grandpa again. He sat on his chair, smiling with his eyes closed. His skin was translucent and baby thin with blue veins pumping through the silver hair on the back of his neck. He looked so fragile. With a flick of the wrist, Tara sent her line back. She could feel the warm sun on her shoulders now, and she envisioned the skirting lure in the water, irresistible; she waited for the line to quicken with a strike.

They fished for a while, everyone together in silence. That silence between them was an understanding, a conversation without speaking. There was only the sound of reels clicking and dock creaking and trees rustling. It was peaceful. But then, like a fire alarm, a shrill voice came from up on the hill, through the screen of trees.

"Yoo-hoo! Where is everybody?" Ruth. In moments, she maneuvered down the slope in her heels and was standing there, hands on hips.

"Well, hello, you two," Ruth said to David and Grandpa, not even glancing at Tara. Grandpa sat up, ran his fingers over his denim shirt to check if it was tucked and buttoned. It wasn't. Ruth eyed Floyd the fish. Gobs of purple blush the color of an old bruise smeared her chubby cheekbones. *She even looks like an evil stepmother,* Tara thought.

"If I'm cooking tonight, I need something to fix. There's nothing in the fridge. Maybe that fish there," Ruth said pointing to Floyd, "or I could thaw out that little chicken from the freezer." And at that, she hoisted the tub to her hip and sloshed back up the slick hill, its path strewn with pine needles. Every few steps, she'd slip, then slide back down a few feet. Each time she lost her footing, she whipped her head back around to see if they saw her blundering. David and Tara looked at each other and suppressed their laughter.

For a moment, Grandpa, with heavy eyelids, watched Ruth's precarious march. Stiff from sitting, he slowly stood, stretched one leg, then the other, remained standing a moment, swayed until he got his balance and hobbled after Ruth to help. He mounted the hill in no time, and, as he stood there for a second, considering if he should really follow Ruth, Tara saw the wind catch his hair, swirling it on end into a Kingfisher's feather crest. She knew he was mustering his strength. Hopefully, he wouldn't lose his breath. That usually happened when he got upset or walked too fast. Tara reeled in her line, her back to the bank and the house, and wondered if Grandpa was just plain tired, the way old men are supposed to be.

"I guess we should go on up," David said. "Just be ready for Mom, OK?"

Tara waited until she heard the screen door slam up at the house, then packed up the tackle box with all the scattered hooks and line and made her way. David carried the poles behind her. She listened as his corduroys swished with his gait as he strode close.

They trekked up the longer, crooked path, switchbacking over the rise. It was all gravel and tree roots, with better footing than the pinestraw trail. Up nearer by the house, they could hear Ruth and Grandpa, the murmur of their voices through soughing branches and sad bird screeches. Just outside the kitchen screen door, Floyd the fish idled in his tub on the cement stoop. The voices from inside were high pitched.

"She can't go skipping school all the time," Ruth said.

"She's a good kid. Just has ideas of her own, that's all," Grandpa said.

David and Tara hid behind an overgrown holly bush; it pricked Tara's arms. Grandpa was starting to wheeze from nerves. This was all her fault.

"You know, we can't drop everything every time she gets in trouble. That's why she's living with you. It was her choice, remember? You gotta take up some of the slack here, if she's gonna stay," Ruth said. Amidst the loud voices, there was the clattering of pots, then the thud of a cabinet closing.

"Maybe you should …. You gotta be patient, Ruth. She's just a kid, and with all the changes …."

Ruth interrupted him mid-sentence. "Look, Henry, I know what it's like to be alone. So, I wanna help her, but your son-in-law and me, well … we won't let any kid, even his, mess up our lives or make it harder."

"It's harder on her," Grandpa said. Tara knew then that Grandpa meant what he was saying, knew he understood. "You know, it's her whole world that's been turned upside down, Ruth … not yours. With her mom gone … then you and Baker going off …." Tara could hear him panting between words. She could feel David eyeing her as she looked down and scribbled ghost designs in the dirt with the toe of her sneaker.

Grandpa gasped for breath, readying himself to go at it another round with Ruth. Then, as the discussion paused, as if suddenly inspired, David leaned the poles he was still holding against the door jamb, grabbed the tackle box from Tara's grip, and burst through the back door. Tara followed. Reluctantly. At the sight of the two, Grandpa and Ruth looked up, embarrassed. David was the first to speak.

"Need any help with dinner?" he asked.

"Not at the moment," said Ruth, glancing at Grandpa, turning her back to them all and facing the stove. Grandpa let out a huge sigh between his staggered breaths. He smiled at Tara, patted her on the shoulder, then shuffled into the den in the canvas sneakers he wore like flips-flops—the back crushed down, yellow heels exposed. Her mother had worn her shoes just the same way. Ruth pushed garlic and tomatoes around a skillet, her back to them still. Tara would let Grandpa settle down, maybe talk to him later. She watched Ruth, noticed Ruth was frowning. She really looked sad.

Spicy scents filled up the place. Dirty dishes, from breakfast and last night's supper, sat crusty with dried eggs and toast all piled in the sink. Tara leaned against the yellow counter and gazed out the kitchen window, while a spider the size of a saucer zigzagged across a new web. David crossed his arms on the kitchen table, his chin down, and piled crumbs from place mats into small mounds. His smooth, brown forearms flexed with each gesture. Tara thought of her mother. She thought of her mother's cooking and the sounds her mother had always made in the kitchen: whistling to herself, reading recipes out loud, singing Judy Garland songs into big metal spoons, making everything fun.

Those days were gone. Now, Tara lived with Grandpa. She'd left her Dad's house soon after he and Ruth got married, soon after Ruth and David moved in. Now that her grandfather was alone, she'd gone to him and asked permission. He had spent so much time nursing Grandma, she wasn't sure if he knew anything else. Tara had visited in those last few days, and she tried to help as Grandpa paced in the kitchen, counted out medicine, made sure all the doses were correct.

Those last days, they worked at changing sheets and moving Grandma's dead weight, all one hundred pounds of it, around the bed when she couldn't move herself. Grandma would smile, but she couldn't muster speech. Sometimes she held her limp, perfectly manicured hand out for Tara to hold, but the festering smells of infection and used adult diapers overwhelmed the small, tender moments.

On the day Grandma died, Grandpa pulled Tara outside to the stoop. It was right before he dripped the last dose of morphine into Grandma's orange juice.

"Was it this bad for Natalie?" he asked.

"No, it wasn't this bad at all," Tara assured him. He blinked twice, his tired, red eyes taking in her answer, scanning her face for more.

"Not this bad at all," she said again. He'd nodded, squeezed her shoulder.

"You stay out here awhile, OK?" Grandpa said, then tried a smile and went back inside. But really, her mother's illness had been bad, very bad, much worse. She hadn't known what to say, so she'd lied about how it felt to watch her mother die. How could she tell him the truth? His wife was dying on his daughter's coattails. Tara didn't need to tell him anything.

It was a little over a year ago that Tara's Mom died. Her last days were the same as Grandma's—the wheezing, the gasping for air, the hollering pains in the middle of the night, the bald head. And then, the dying was over and Mom and Grandma and their lives disappeared down a hole as their coffins were lowered out of sight. Tara knew Grandpa must feel as she did—all that emptiness that weighed so heavy. At Grandma's funeral, Tara saw the expression on Grandpa's face. She watched him the whole way back in the funeral limo. As they turned the last corner, she turned to her father. *Dad, you think it's OK if I go stay with Grandpa for a while?*

At home, Tara packed up all her things for Grandpa's, and David, her new stepbrother, tall as a twelfth-grader, leaned in her doorway and watched. He watched her all the time. She didn't mind. Ever since Ruth and her Dad got married, a scant six months after Mom died, ever since David moved in, he'd taken to watching her. Sometimes she felt some new sensation when he watched her or walked by. Sometimes just his smile as he burst out of the bathroom or his simple "Morning" as they passed in the hall would make her stomach twist like a key turning in a lock. And when he settled into the house after moving in, David instantly became her ally at the supper table. He laughed at all her silly jokes, while Dad sat and screwed up his puzzled face, and Ruth, always in the kitchen doing something, would hear the laughter and step into the room, wiping her hands on her apron.

"What'd I miss?" Ruth would ask. Tara would look at David and he'd wink.

"Nothing, Mom," he'd say and smile at Tara between bites of chicken. Tara's stomach always turned at dinner. She never finished a meal with David around.

But, despite David, Grandpa needed her. She knew it. And she liked her new freedom, anyway. She had a cot and a little room off the study—a "sleeping porch" is what Grandpa liked to call it. It was fine staying with Grandpa. Better than her old house. Though it was only twenty miles north of Dad and Ruth, it felt like a continent away.

☾

Every night, in Tara's new world, from her window in her sleeping porch, she saw and heard things she could never see and hear at home. She listened to crickets and watched the silhouettes of bats skitter across the lake, and then before she knew it, she'd fall into a deep, comfortable sleep. The lullaby of wood owls and buzzing bugs drew her deep and away from her heavy loneliness.

When she was far down into those dreams, wonderful things happened that she couldn't remember later, and it was hard to wake up come the morning and the alarm clock, hard to make that first bell at school. Grandpa usually let her snooze. Especially when she'd been talking in her sleep. She couldn't remember those dream conversations. But she knew that her mother was in there, somewhere in the deep.

Tara sighed as she stood in the kitchen with her memories. Leaning right there against the counter she could try to let herself remember those dreams. And then Ruth's voice snapped her out of it

"I guess if you two really wanna help, you can go clean that fish," Ruth said, breaking the long silence. She waved the spatula like a baton. David stood and grabbed Tara's elbow off the counter.

"Come on, we gotta earn our keep," he said and winked at her. Tara let David lead her out back.

In the tub, Floyd the fish still hovered in the muddy water, his gills whiffling in fits and starts.

"He doesn't look so good," David said.

"It's sad," Tara said.

"Think we should let him go?"

"Your mom'll be pissed."

"She can thaw out that chicken."

And at that, they both smiled and grabbed a handle, made a run for it, laughing all the way down the slippery hill, the water sploshing everywhere.

On the dock, Tara snatched up Floyd, but the fish, he wriggled through her fingers and flopped across the wood planking. David and Tara both swiped in vain, while Floyd thrashed about in wild, slimy fits. He moved closer to the edge by degrees, until, in one great splash, Floyd writhed off the dock—*Kerr-Plunk!*—and, in the water, he hesitated, then swayed in the turgid current, unsure of his sudden freedom. Finally, as if he had to think about it, Floyd made his exit as he dashed between two Styrofoam pontoons.

David and Tara's shoulders touched. David fixed on the point where Floyd went under. He bit his lip.

"You wanna go swimming?" he asked.

"We don't have suits."

He laughed, stripped down to his boxers, his clothes a heap of color on the dock, red and blue, then dove in. She followed. The water was bracing, and, as she surfaced, she crossed her arms over her bra and small breasts, with her hands tucked into her armpits, and kicked her feet to stay afloat. The little fish down there, a little bigger than tadpoles, licked at her toes.

David swam under, brushing up between her shoulder blades as he surfaced like a dolphin. He sliced out far then, skirted the point and vanished out past the bend. With a fast crawl, she chased and tried to catch him, and when she finally caught up, she found him bobbing in the cove, waiting. She, too, bobbed for a while she faced the shore, faced away from the center of the lake, then floated on her back in circles, arms and legs splayed, and gazed up at gray sheets of cloud marbled with moisture. David kicked white plumes of water over her.

"If you get tired, I'll hold onto you," David said.

"OK, I'm getting there."

From the cabin, they heard Ruth, then Grandpa, beckon—*Da-vid! Tar-a! Come to dinn-er!* They pretended not to hear, paddled around each other, spat water through pursed lips. It tasted like copper pennies.

They settled somewhere in the middle of the lake, in a warm spot they happened upon. A breeze puffed above them through the pines and the birds whispered in twilight song. Tara treaded through black lace reflections of tree foliage strewn across the lake's surface. Up and down, up and down. And then, not really tired or anything, she sidestroked over to David, took him up on his offer, draped her arms over his shoulders, wrapped her legs around his waist. The lock clicked open in her stomach as she watched the drips sparkle on the tips of his eyelashes. He held her like that with little effort.

"Guess we're having that chicken after all," David said. She giggled, and he squeezed her tight at the ribs.

"You know," David said, "Everything's lighter in water."

She did know. Entwined, they drifted like that for a long time, buoyed together, ignoring the adults' calls as they echoed through the trees and all across the lake, and a crescent moon scratched at the horizon.

PART II

HISTORY IS A GALLERY
OF PICTURES

History is filled with the sound of silken slippers going downstairs and wooden shoes coming up.

—Voltaire

It is an odd thing, but everyone who disappears is said to be seen at San Francisco. It must be a delightful city, and possess all the attractions of the next world.

—Oscar Wilde

We are hardly permanent. The bacteria in our guts are more permanent. Summer's pond scum is older by time spans we cannot fathom: the elder cyanobacteria are 3.5 billion years old.

—Christopher Cokinos, *Hope Is the Thing With Feathers*

History is a gallery of pictures in which there are few originals and many copies.

—Alexis de Tocqueville

HOW CAN YOU
TITLE LONGING?

Remember too
The swelling of the buds,
The waiting for blossoms set to burst,
First signs that summer almost came.

1.

The Witherspoon sisters were good at keeping traditions. They were devoted, proper. They did their chores; they tended their home. They were ever mindful of their town standing.

On Saturdays, they dried their white stockings in the dark room off the kitchen. After returning from town trips, they restrung their rope pearls to prevent their necklaces' silk floss from turning a dingy brown. In sweltering summers, they hushed their bright windows with gauze, scrimming the heat. During particularly cold winters, they sprinkled lye to unfreeze the house's drainpipes. They were always appropriate. But this is not the sisters' story.

The youngest of the three, Violet, is the one who deserves our attention here; she was the most diligent, the most interesting. Violet Gray Witherspoon did much more than tend politesse or duties. She felt things deeply and acted upon them. Her life was not one of excitement, but one day she scribbled the name "John Josiah Chambers" on rose-scented paper. After she inscribed his name in her fine calligraphy, she concealed the scrap of paper at the bottom of the button box and hid it in the back of the sewing closet. But hiding it didn't mean that she forgot why she had done something so scandalous, for when she was alone, she twiddled the man's name over and over with her tongue: "John Josiah Chambers. John Josiah Chambers." While snapping beans for dinner or when she folded the laundry off the line, she caressed the words of his name around her mouth.

The name stayed with her, but Violet did nothing about it. And she had never asked God for much. Of course, like every good Baptist, she'd often prayed for fine weather or for plentiful harvests. Now, though, she found herself begging the Almighty for a chance to slip away with a man she barely knew.

The creeks ran over. It was spring. And Violet napped fitfully on her four-poster bed. She hoped her shallow dreams would dull the longing and quell the strange ache in her belly, a pain she was not accustomed to having. Ladies in her family did not nap, but she tried to doze, anyway.

Etta Mae from the quilting bee noticed Violet's absences that spring, and when Violet made a rare attendance at their Wednesday afternoon gatherings, Etta Mae remarked on her friend's unusual color. Violet's listless eyes drew concern. Attributing Violet's symptoms to seasonal love, she counseled, "Open your mouth every other kiss. He'll love you more, or he won't love you at all." Violet smiled. She could only dream of knowing closeness.

Following routines was life. Other than the usual housekeeping, Violet walked to town on family errands every Monday and Friday (the general store, the feed store, hardware, butcher, and baker). Sometimes, for excitement, she reached inside her handkerchief drawer to slide on her finest kid gloves, the ones she usually reserved for dances and formal affairs. She pushed the everyday moleskins to the back and laughed at her frivolity.

Think of the fingers that wore those dressy gloves: impossibly tiny, the knuckles like charms, a grasp that later wrote pained poetry. Think about the adolescent who carried on after her parents died; ruminate on the helpful child who grew into an adult, a young lady who assisted her old-maid sisters and bachelor brother. Think of her in the enchanted land of the Deep South with its verdant humidity all honeysuckle sweet, its lightning storms in fall, its thunder drumming away summers.

Think of how she lost each of her beloved siblings to a terrible fate: the influenza epidemic, a gun accident (her brother, Henry, shot through the forehead as he cleaned his own pistol), a fall down the stairs; they all went to the grave until she was the only one left living in that huge house on the corner.

Yet Violet carried on. Imagine the pain of the hands that could not hold what they wanted. Imagine how in town at the butcher's week after week, she saw her crush, John Josiah Chambers, and, when she finally arrived home alone, how she would toss off her gloves and forget to remove her hat, how she'd write poem after poem, sometimes taking months to perfect her rhymes. And every Sabbath before she went to Sunday school alone, she'd stand in front of the cheval glass, adjust her special hat with the dangling cherries, arrange her long pearls, then tug on the little gloves (oh, the vanity of a less-than-beautiful woman!). She'd cover her hands grown coarse over time, hands that had mended tears, darned socks, shucked corn, scrubbed floors, and scraped chamber pots; hands that had worked away stains from grungy sheets, phlegm-crusted handkerchiefs, and menstrual rags. She'd covered her hands. She'd covered them and hoped.

2.

At the flea market, under a stack of romance novels, a shopper finds a slender collection of poetry. It's embossed with gold letters. The linen cover is the green of a deep, mysterious oak forest. The title, *Lest You Forget*, is dramatic, and the book sports a scarlet ribbon wagging from the spine like a trail of tender sumac. A photograph of the author is dated 1888 and is adhered to the frontispiece with dusty colored photo album corners. In the picture, a proper lady stares at the camera with sad eyes. And if a reader delves between the covers, he or she will discover romantic yearnings, unusual thoughts for such a staid-looking woman. They are not improper, but they're close. And these poems never offended anyone while the poet was alive: The book did not go to print until more than fifty years after she had passed, when a greedy granddaughter went hunting and discovered a folio in the back of a sewing closet.

The poet's full name is printed in a sweeping vine cursive script on the dedication page: VIOLET GRAY WITHERSPOON. Such a descriptive name. All nouns. All real, concrete things. Violet: a small, sweetly fragrant flower, a harbinger of spring. Gray: a non-color that calls to mind boredom and the hats men once wore to church but always removed before entering. Wither: the fading of blooms (violets, perhaps?). Spoon: the shape of domesticity, a symbol of comfort, a tool for scooping pudding. Violet. Gray. Witherspoon. All of these names and images evoke the woman who is described in the poetry book's prologue notes.

So after examining this book of poems, close it, then open it once more. Peer at the photograph; notice the face! A small, flippy nose; smooth, buttery skin; soaring cheekbones; a sturdy jaw; bee-stung lips—shiny from nervous licking, no doubt. Eyes, light and large, that seem to drift past the photographer to another place. Tight, white Victorian collar clasped to the side with a twinkling bar pin; a curl of lace caressing the lady's prominent chin where it ends after wrapping so delicately around her long nape. And the hair—so fluffy in its upswept nest.

Nothing in this early photo makes us see Violet's artistic intentions. We see a good daughter, yes, and a future wife. A mother who will be dutiful and handsome. Ah, there is such devotion in her expression. No, Violet Gray Witherspoon was not the sort of woman who turned heads at cotillions, but this young woman's good bones will lend her a stately air in her old age. She will not turn spoon-shaped like her name. All of this is captured forever in the present moment of this photo.

So what can we really know? One thing's for sure: Violet did not die without knowing how it felt to have a man tickle his nails down her spine. She certainly knew that there are scratches in this world that satisfy, but they usually leave a mark.

3.

Secrets there are within my soul,
Secrets that breathe only in the lightest moments
When all about is sombre, safe, and even cold.

'Tis then they soar to heights unfathomed.
In private moments, my secrets live a life
*   that never faces death from disappointment,*
A life that flies into a sky of stars
*   years of lives away.*
Free have been my secrets,
Free to dream, to dip, to soar where ere they may.
Whst! A word calls them to task.
How dreadful that my secrets cannot last!

"In this book are thirty-three poems written by a woman who lived her entire life in Macon, Georgia," the preface states. "Violet Witherspoon was not a prolific writer. Mostly her work included poems, stories, and a sporadic journal of isolated events."

Imagine her family amongst the first wave of settlers in middle Georgia, mid-seventeenth or eighteenth century, a good English-descended family who stuck it out through the Civil War, who owned one or two slaves and were kind to them, who set them free before abolition (one tries to believe this of anyone who lived in Georgia at this time—but who can know?). The family resided in a large, two-story white house, and the bay window faced south on a corner plot; they had a water pump in their back yard, blighted gardenia bushes bordering the garden, clematis vines climbing their porch trellis, and they made peach ice cream on Sundays with just the right amount of agar and ice they'd bought down at the general store in Macon town proper.

Violet's poems are not titled. How can you title longing? Numbers are easier to discard. She did write one journal entry about her poems—"My work has suffered due to lack of time and lack of talent, but nothing has suffered as much as my skill in the domestic arts. My fingers have always been maladroit with needlework. Many a friend has produced dazzling quilts in wonderful patches of color or embroidered magnificent rose bouquets or created rich, overflowing vegetable gardens. Not me."

Violet was good at imagining, though. And she knew the town would not permit what she had dreamt about every day—an unbalanced match, Violet and John Josiah. Such an inferior union would scandalize the memory of her sisters and brother and ruin the family name. Her sisters had reminded her often when they were alive: "Respectability will feed you. Love will not."

4.

To gather up the winds and waters of the world
        with open-fingered hands,
To vision into blackness of the night
        with sightless eyes,
  To spin my being into timeless, airless space
        for passion's sake:
Such is the longing for my Distant Spirit,
        harvester of my past,
        taker of tomorrow's dreams,

my untouched phantom
whose half-illumined visage, like the moon,
circles 'round me slowly,
 deepening purple shadows,
weaving shrouds to wrap my soul.

A spinster. A woman who has never married. This is not Violet. She was more than a spinster, far more. She did not die an old maid; she was a bearer, a keeper of feelings that no one but the page would ever know. And when her aloneness was forgotten, the paper always remembered. Oh, the sadness in this poetry. Violet loved John Josiah. They were engaged, but something happened. We do not know what. Perhaps there was a scene that precipitated rejection. Maybe it was simple, childish.

It was a weekday. She dropped by his office with a small potted plant, a miniature camellia with dark pink blooms, waxy, not fragrant. It was a masculine flower, if there is such a thing. She wrapped the clay pot in green tissue, knotted the bow to perfection. But John Josiah did not smile when his assistant opened the office door, and, though her demeanor was only kind, mannered, Violet was spirited away. She had done nothing improper, no. But somehow she had offended him.

And so, as she departed John Josiah's accounting firm, she darted one last glance through the closing mahogany door. She spied her fiancé's dark hair drooping over an eye, his tight waistcoat and rolled-up shirtsleeves pushed above his elbows with homemade garters. She'd always admired his strong forearms and sallow tallness. After the door slammed, she heard a laugh and a muffled crash as the pot hit the bottom of the dustbin. Afterwards, for hours, she sat on a park bench in the town square.

After that day, John Josiah Chambers never called on Violet again. He married another. And less than a year after his grand wedding, the first wife went to the ground. And then the scoundrel married again. Surely, all the while he was with his wives, he regretted his treatment of the lovely woman who had given him a flowering plant.

5.

Now the poems are all we possess of Violet's half-century of yearning. Yet something happened during the time of his second marriage—it is evident in Violet's poems from that period. The tone shifts. The shy poetess somehow changed her world.

One bright day, when the cloudy mirror glass sparkled and jangled, Violet was no longer examining herself for church. No. She was finally acting. She unclasped her leather-gloved fingers from her bosom, hired a cab, and, in sticky late-autumn heat, traveled miles on the dusty roads. And when she reached her destination, she stepped onto the clay road and sent the carriage away. She gingerly walked to the back door of the house, then tiptoed inside, where she dropped her hat and linen coat to the dining room floor, loosened her spiraled hair, and then John Josiah came down the stairs to greet her and used his sweet lips and teeth to peel off those exquisite gloves, finger by finger, before he captured her in his arms, and, in a snowy squall of undergarments, he rushed her away from all the troubles she'd known, and the pink, wild roses climbed the eaves outside, and the light augered through the oak branches, and she smiled, content, as she heard a fly buzzing at the window, or maybe it was a moth or even the spirits of unborn children who were pushing at her cavity to enter, and then, in a delirious pause, John Josiah fetched one of those fine gloves and sighed and relented and transformed the little thing into a womb. In her fever, Violet promised herself something she would later regret. She would never wear those gloves again.

Her warm home held memories. Every late afternoon, just so she could return home anew, she'd stroll to the store to purchase fresh milk and bread. How inviting were the lights of the big Witherspoon house as she turned the last corner!

It was a temperate early December, and her light overcoat and lace-ups were comfortable for the season. Violet wore a Christmas wreath pin on her lapel. Holiday shoppers filled the sidewalks: Fat grandmothers wore feathered hats, tired maids checked items off their long lists, sniffling children played tag and hid behind trees and bushes, a scruffy street sweeper leaned against a lamppost with a broom at his feet. Violet wobbled and weaved as she balanced her parcels and bags all twined together—Christmas somethings for the neighbor's children, green food dye for spritzer cookies, milk, and bread. She walked beneath the low-hanging limbs of the undressed trees above her, the leaves long gone to November, and she smiled, thinking about how beautiful the branches were in their deciduous bareness. Yet she also knew that permanent barrenness was decidedly not beautiful. It was something altogether different.

And then somehow the truth hit her: Her blood had not flowed since that one afternoon she'd spent with John Josiah Chambers. And that was far worse than his disdain for her—he had not once acknowledged her when she passed his family's pew at church.

The bright sunlight turned over, and pale afternoon darkness shadowed the sky like a narrow leaf blown across the eyes. The rain came. The first drop touched the side of her head, and small, close sounds caressed her. Gentle rain thickened fescue in the yards. She pushed at her silk umbrella, but it would not open, and the rain kept coming, and her thin packages sogged through. She lifted her head back, gave in to the wetness falling harder now, and closed her eyes. The drenched trees gave off their pleasant petrichor and perfumed the rain. She imagined the rag doll for Lily, the Wilsons' child, swelling up like a sponge, its face distending into a ghoulish expression. The new food dye would fall through its wet box to the sidewalk, breaking and spilling, a long, emerald trickle seeping down to the roots of the town's live oaks. When she opened her eyes, the road had thickened into a clay soup in the downpour, and just then a little single horse carriage pulled alongside her. The small bay horse nickered and a gentleman spoke.

"Ma'am, can I help?" From underneath the carriage's canvas cover, a handsome man, no more than forty, touched the brim of his hat. His voice was warm, like her home.

It was already August, and the last of the strawberry preserves cooled on the windowsill. In the sharp slant of morning light, the jars glowed like garnet gems, the scarlet of birth and death. Archer Beauregard Tuttle was out in the vegetable patch, tying up tomato plants. He'd never know the truth, or maybe he'd always known it and cared not to think about it. Nevertheless, he didn't mention his suspicions to his new wife about the child who was due any day. Such a kind man!

As Violet went about her mending, she propped her work on her bulging belly. She hoped for a daughter. And while she worked on her husband's socks, she could not fathom why she had passed so many years longing for someone else. Why had she cared to write a man's name on the slip of paper that she just discovered in the bottom of the button box? Her compulsion to write was long gone; her poems did not buzz at her ears anymore. The happiness she felt would not allow the rhymes to come.

6.

… The late day nods; its chin droops
in an old man's doze;
it mulls our callow talk of this tomorrow.

At summer's close,
I grieve the once-bright colors
*   faded now to neutral shades*
And rue the abandonment of our sweet September days.

Oh, Violet, was it your secret that kept you from writing? After Archer died on the road where you'd met him, why didn't you shed one tear? All through your later years, during those long nights, the biggest stars looked at you, and every night when the pines swayed in the wind and starlight and sang another man's name with their leaves of wire, did the three words haunt you? They still haunt your poetry. John Josiah Chambers.

Archer is gone. So are you. But Olivia Tuttle, your daughter, lived on. And the slip of paper with John Josiah's name remained at the bottom of the button box where your daughter kept it hidden, though she did not know why.

Propriety. Obligation. Tradition. We've read your book, Violet. We want more. We wish you had gone back to your secret love and your forbidden desires. Gone back to caring about respectability. Prayed for your loved ones in alphabetical order, hung your white stockings in the dark, sprinkled lye in winter, hushed the windows with muslin, restrung your long pearls. Gone back to turning over your house's mattresses, turning your bed to face the east for good luck, turning your house inside out as the moon spun and waltzed in reverie to the trees' three-word song. Turning new pages over and over. Turning over in your last slumber, your ghost hiding your child's truth.

We wish you had written more.

SMASH THE TEACUPS,
STORM THE SKY

What about the fire? It threw a great heat across the room, all the way to the edges, to the singed velvet drapes where she stood. It burned with surging snaps and swelled high inside the fireplace. Its incandescence turned all the wooden stretchers to shadow, and one by one it licked the painted faces. The pyre smoldered black, sallowed the color in the paintings' high cheeks; it combusted the furrowed brows, erased smooth foreheads, crackled scarlet mouths. And all the rendered eyes the artist had so carefully created? The blaze caressed and kindled them as they went down, their sad gazes flaming out. They blinked. The fire took the eyes last.

The artist, no longer a young woman, already a grandmother, tossed in work after work, and the coruscations climbed a ladder of warm hues, first yellow, then orange until they reached the brightest rung of red. Unfortunately, the blind artist saw none of the spectacle.

☾

Earlier that day, the artist's chauffeur, who was named Philippe, drove her through the outskirts of the city; it was a fine morning, and the car bumped along in a soft rhythm. And then the artist spotted color in the fields.

"Pull over." Her command came in her native English, the drawl still decidedly Southern. The chauffeur reacted slowly, but she wouldn't tolerate his hesitance—she poked her head over the partition and spoke again, this time sharply.

"Pull over, I say!" In a measured steer, he guided the long auto onto the shoulder, the tires furrowing the long grass.

"Help me out … please." She spoke in a more gentle register now.

So he carried her from the cab and she stood in a field amongst early fall lilies, their bright crimson buzzing in the mid-morning light. She inhaled and found the air redolent of peat fire, a muddy smell from far off. And then she directed her eyes down to her feet, tried to focus on a colorful smudge there. No eyeglasses were needed for this; she could identify the flower by smell. She plucked it, brought it close to her face. Still, no, no, she could not focus—she still could not make out the details.

"*Bon!*" She grabbed for her chauffeur's elbow as he moved her back into her seat. She pulled the flower to her nose and sniffed its sweetness, then held it inches from her lashes. But the lily was only a smear—still no definition. She could not make out any petals or stamens or even the stem. She frowned as she looked out the window, but then consoled herself. At least she could still see colors! The field was blood red; it was the vermilion of locomotive cabooses or of a baby's clammy lips. The grass was the green calm of a deep sea. She tucked the flower into her bun, tapped the driver's seat with her stick, and closed her eyes as the car purred towards Paris.

The Louvre was a fine place. High walls, very white. Great looming windows for light. On the cold floors, her hard-soled shoes tapped out soft echoes that bounced back to her in even softer whispers. The galleries were church-quiet with just the murmur of her steps and the occasional yelp or shout from people on the street outside.

In the museum, she knew the way by heart, was sure of where she was walking. She paced through room after room until she found, by memory, what she'd come for. There it was. Her favorite: Jacques-Louis David. She leaned in close to the large painting, the gold of the frame sparkling in a slit of light from the windows high above. This painting was an old friend she'd admired many times in her youth, and though she knew that it depicted some gory battle scene, she now only saw the opalescence of flesh tones and a ruby drip here or there. Perhaps the color she now saw was a burgundy robe or a disembow-eled peasant. Perhaps it was a harem lady's mantle or an Oriental rug. No matter, the colors were rich, and that was what she liked. And the sky! She remembered that there was a turbulent, majestic sky in this painting.

That day, not another soul walked through the lower corners of the Louvre, so she had the masterpiece to herself. She paused, listened, and then knew she what she must do. Without a second thought, she tilted her head forward. Closer. Closer. She waited for a reprimand from a guard. But there was only silence. Unconcerned now that someone would stop her, she carefully leaned in and pressed her nose toward the canvas until it gave a little like soft flesh, and, with a long stroke, she licked the painting. Her tongue swiped softness, the texture smooth as a calm wind. She could also discern the slight grain of brush strokes. There was the taste of brine, a slight tinge of the Mediterranean on a hot day. Dark waves, strong waves flashed through her memory, sharks surfaced and glinted in the high sunlight. Oh yes, she tasted the sea on her tongue.

She stood for a while close to the painting, and though she was late for an appointment, she knew people would wait for her. She walked for a bit, dallied, leaned on a column next to a few fine sculptures. The statues' shapes were undefined, imprecise to her eyes—hulking stone figures on pedestals. She watched their lurking silhouettes change color in the sunlight for over an hour, and all the while, the saltwater taste of the painting lingered in her mouth, made her uncommonly happy. She purled it around her gums as she finally made her way back through the museum, volitant, tapping, her thin hand twittling atop her walking stick, her white hair pulled back under a brightly crocheted cap. One more errand and she could be home by afternoon.

☾

The fire took the canvases which stretched tight as pelts; they burned and sank into themselves. She tossed each one in with an eagerness for the loss. With this conflagration, there was no going back. Sketches, drawings, studies, Salon paintings. It didn't matter. From her glory days, there were mothers nursing babies, women writing letters, girls lounging about. Oh, such ugly, ladylike paintings. Soon, it would all be soot. Burn it all. Smash the damned teacups!

She flung off her shawl, and through the stiff swelter, she could hear the blaze as it jigged and hissed, begging for more. Now it was time to give the inferno her early works: robust women playing mandolins, Goya copies, Velázquez replicas. Muted browns and cadmium reds.

And the men, too. She'd throw those in now, the poor dears. She'd painted them early on. She'd never seen a lack in her masculine renderings, but no one had wanted these. Perhaps she had never understood men. After all, she *had* missed moments—her husband's pillow was cold only months after their ceremony, and she had never relished caring for him in health let alone sickness; she had never soaped his sore back or rubbed his tired, calloused feet. She'd had other men, but they had not mattered. And her own children were useless things; she did not care one wit where they had gone or if they were even still living.

Other things bothered her. There were many glorious things that she had never been allowed to paint. She had wanted to depict epic battles, stormy-skied backdrops, foreground armies besieging gates, and middle-ground

generals rearing back on horses. Instead, she had per-
fected sunshine and the peace and mathematics in drawing rooms. She had honed lines. Mastered draftsmanship
and the composition in soft fabrics. Balanced light and
dark on children's cheeks, color and its absence at tea
parties. Poppycock.

Now, the bonfire pushed high, greedy for more. Her
fingers searched along the wall and found her easel
propped against the jamb; she tried to crack it in half over
her stiff knee, but she only bruised herself, so she pitched
it in whole. And then she found one of her famous pieces,
and it became her final fuel. Good-bye, you silly lady sip-
ping tea! It sailed into the heat, lost forever to cinders.

At midday, after her visit to the Louvre, Philippe drove
her masterfully through the Paris streets and maneuvered
the car between two poles at the dealer's storefront. Her
head now throbbed in the bright light, so the kind chauffeur steadied her, pushed open the shop door. When a
voice greeted her from a dark corner, she entered the tight
room and straightened; she could not see the speaker.
Though she was not one to frown, she did not smile either.

"Ah, you came after all! I was hoping you brought …."
He spoke to her in English. She cut him off.

"No paintings today," she replied.

"But why come?" the dealer asked. And before the artist
could think about it, she lied.

"I've destroyed them." Until that very moment, she had
not known what she would say to the dealer, nor what she'd

do with her paintings. For days, she had worried about what to do, and her latest works crouched in the corner of her studio, covered with a sheet, hiding in shame, waiting for her decision. They were hideous monsters.

Oh, she was tired.

"Pour quoi? They are *all* destroyed?" The dealer's voice was panicked.

"All of them. Into the fire." She shrugged and pointed toward the dealer's diminutive fireplace where crackling embers warmed the stone hearth where she stood. That afternoon, she'd had no plan for her ugly creations until she felt the heat of the small blaze on her legs. And then she knew what she must do. She was done. No more— even if the dealer (as she remembered, the ugly man had always appeared so unkempt with his messy handlebar mustache pointing to heaven, his wrinkled linen waist-coat, and his sweaty palms) had promised her even more wealth. He had visited often, bowing repeatedly as he tried to convince her of her importance; he was too young to know that his sycophancy was offensive.

"Important buyers … from overseas … your reputa-tion … *je ne sais quoi … qu'est-ce que c'est? Alors,* Madame, *vous êtes,* you are a … master." Why the insult of beseech-ing her in his poorly enunciated English? Everyone in the world knew that she spoke French as well as any Parisian.

She deserved respect. She'd earned her stature, her opinions, and her wiry countenance, too.

☾

The fireplace gave off a powerful shine; the hewn stone mantel glowed. Because she could not really see them, she imagined the flames defeating the paint, leaping off the faces in victory, crawling and pinking over backgrounds, satins, and silks, bouncing and tearing the tufted upholsteries she'd so carefully fashioned with her brush. And, as the combustion curled around the last remnants, hungry for more, she heard her *pince-nez* pop, the glass bursting at just the right temperature. She'd thrown those in after the fact. She didn't need to see anymore, and the eyeglasses didn't help much anyway. She was blind and nothing would change that.

She stood in the corner of the room, the ashes lifting in the grate, pushing up through the flue. The singed fetor seeped into her clothes, into her nose hairs, into every fissure of the chateau's grounds. It sulked up the stairs to the servant's quarters.

The stench brought Clemence, her maid, racing down the back stairs into the studio.

"Oh, Madame! *Pour quoi? Pour quoi?*" The maid's hands flew through the air like scared birds and her voice filled the room with grief.

The artist tightened her lips and walked away and out the side door. She would walk all the way to Paris if she wanted. But which way was north? And was she still even on the footpath? She lifted her skirt, misjudged the distance over a stone and stumbled, then tripped on a fallen limb. She brushed off her bruised knee and stood again. She had lost her way. And she knew then that no matter how much she wanted to escape, she could not make it far.

Her life's work was gone; it hovered in the light wind. All her paintings were only the scent of burnt fabric and oil, and their residue coated her blouse and hair, grit stuck up under her nails. She waded into the high grass of the meadow and past the corn and vegetables she had brought from her home in Georgia. Then she found a log and sat, sniffing at the dusty air.

Behind her in the dark woods, a stream whispered, as if it was a liquid voice in an opened tomb. She couldn't make out the words, but the sound of the water was fraught with yearning and something else, some other sound in the background, a soft rustling. The fluorescence of wild-flowers was all around her; it calmed her.

She gazed sightless to where the stream emptied into the green pond, and she was sure that she could see two swans—no, three—bright in the late afternoon sun. They drifted like shadowy ballerinas upon the surface of water, floodlit in the winnowing light. She closed her eyes, and yet she could still see their ghostly after-images pirouette and leap over the canvas of her eyelids. Their white dance blazed, clear and bright as anything she had ever seen.

All the Birds in Shakespeare

The bluebird carries the sky on his back.
—Henry David Thoreau

It came down to who owned the air. These birds took away even the clouds, usurping such thick azure skies. Never mind bluebirds, songbirds, woodpeckers, and flickers, all of them displaced, nudged out of nests, habitats ruined. Where do all the small birds go? But house sparrows don't care, nor starlings, for that matter.

Starlings fly mean—their dominant, raucous cackles loud and coarse, as dozens soar down to nest in hazes of young ash and pine. These birds. Descendants of eighty avian beasts shipped from Europe. Their first stop in the invasion? A mass release in Central Park on March 9, 1890, by some man named Eugene Spatzmeister. Good old Eugene. It all happened innocently enough, one imagines.

He was old. He was rich. But one assumes he was not happy. Those types never are. Eugene did not make a real mark, after all, unless selling liquor up and down the Eastern Seaboard is a contribution. His business is still around. Look it up. Poor Eugene. How would he know that he was ruining something he'd never even heard of: ecology? Good intentions lead to hell. Does anyone ever worry about poor, homeless birds?

One thing about Eugene, he was good at decisions. He resolved months before that historic day in March to do his adopted country a favor. He'd deliver birds across the big pond. Only a few were needed here in America, really, though Shakespeare mentioned over six hundred species in his sonnets and plays. America had plenty of birds. Swan, cock, robin, swallow, wren, lark and thrush. To name a few. Of the long list that our friend, the fastidious Eugene, compiled, only a small number weren't natives.

Eugene himself heard tell often of buntings, spied turkeys and buzzards every few days in the country; he'd even eavesdropped on the loving coos of mourning doves whilst tromping about his estate, shotgun in hand. So, Eugene devised a master plan. It wouldn't be difficult to execute. He had the money, the time. What was the harm? Reading the genius Bard night after night sparked the idea for the whole thing: Any civilized country should have all the birds of Shakespeare soaring about its skies.

Envisage the scene: Eugene waiting at the docks in New York as the crates came in. It could've been a foggy, late-winter morning, with long, thick ropes creaking as they threaded through rusting pulleys. There was probably loud cussing, too, from the shoremen in caps unloading the ship. Eugene stood there on the dock, perhaps, with his chauffeur, who never called him anything but "sir"— this chauffeur, probably his only friend. And then they heard the birds singing, trilling, lilting, flittering about in wooden boxes bigger than fifteen coffins as they lowered to shore. Maybe the sun burnt off the early morning fog at that very moment.

"Birds?" asked his surprised driver and attendant, his sometimes confidant, Jackey Collins, the man's usual Irish obsequiousness absent.

"Yes," answered Eugene as he smoothed his fingers across the top of his bald, hatless head and plucked the soft wax at the tips of his thick mustache, the ends curling toward his cold ears like serifs. "Yes. Birds." The answer was solid, firm, the words monosyllabic. As usual, as always.

So that auspicious day, the day the birds finally arrived, Jackey drove his employer in a lorry carriage stacked high with twirping crates to the middle of the park, stationed the wagon there on a hill, a little knob of land, and Eugene had the honor of sliding open each heavy lid, unlatching every wire cage, releasing demise, spawning witches. Oh, he set the villains free! The creatures took wing in the park, dimmed the mohair blue sky, its cabinet of clouds, while flashes of bird tail and beak reflected in Eugene's black patent boots as they flew out on their mission. One by one, each bird lifted its menace into the afternoon, tracing out spells with broomstick wings across this new foreign land. And one by one, they hovered in the virgin wind, then went up, up, up, warbling as they lofted, until Eugene could never imagine or want to see anything else. Air does not discriminate.

The starling was one transplant. The worst by far. It was also Eugene's favorite bird from his home so far away. Those starlings with their slick darkness like well-dressed demons, small enchantresses, they squatted in other birds' homes. That didn't matter to Eugene. No, he loved their grouping nature, the way they clung to one another as if they were one, big flying machine, they could frill to places, elevating above everything, traveling where he could not. To the sky! To the air, a place so dark and luminous at twilight, with skittering bugs to eat; come dawn, that same pitted heaven transformed itself into a dazzling sanctuary, brightening into a blazing pink backdrop for the avian world as they perched in silhouettes on old trees, the thick branches comfortable for so many to rest upon.

After the release, Eugene dreamt of nothing but feathers and beaks and wings and little yellow feet. The birds kept him up at night. He congratulated himself often. And he was certain that someday he would hear coveys with their collaborative mechanism outside his lonesome, blue window, a future-swarm of thousands (his progeny, of sorts) would glide by. He knew one day that he'd peer at them through his mother-of-pearl opera glasses; the chattering racket would deafen him from all those backwards beaks.

Then, one particular nightfall, something extraordinary happened. The evening started like every other, with Eugene preening himself with reminiscences—*Oh! Old William would be so happy with my gift to this barren country!* And, as usual, the soft cloud of sleep weighed down upon the old man's eyelids as he sipped through his second brandy, his finger poking his place in the new collected works of the master playwright, the book inches thick and leather bound.

Later, his companion-chauffeur, Jackey, would find his employer's place marked with a peacock feather in that same volume, the tome's printing oblong and punctuated with little, delicate flourishes like chicken scratches or the shadows of tiny leaves. For many years after, Jackey would often recite the saved passage to his grandchildren to try to make sense of it all. A few lines were his only clue, from *Macbeth*, Act IV, Scene II:

Lady Macduff: What had he done, to make him
      fly the land?

Ross: You must have patience, madam.

Lady Macduff: He had none;
      His flight was madness.
      When our actions do not,
      Our fears do make us traitors.

No one ever found Eugene Spatzmeister after that fateful night. Did they look? He left no trace, after all, but the open book on his favorite chair and the empty snifter and one oxblood slipper, upside down, forgotten on the flagstones, outside and below.

As for Eugene himself, he would never remember what he was reading at his vanishing, nor would he feign to care. But he would, over and over, muse about that terrible nightmare he had, waking only to find himself scudding into another, deeper dream, the time when he dangled on the windowsill and then shuttlecocked down, ass over teakettle, until there was a rustle of featherless debris, brittle as moths' wings, until he lifted, exalted, through a scribble of cirrus clouds, the spokes of light from all the stars trembling as he mounted the wind. He would remember that. The flocks of birds would come later. Together they would pull him up into countless murmurations. Up and up. Ascending. Always up.

THIRTY MEN, NOT ONE

No more painters, no more scribblers ... no more religions ... no more nations ... an end at last to all this stupidity, nothing left, nothing at all, nothing, nothing.

—*Louis Aragon, from the "Manifesto of the Dada Movement," 1918*

Dada. It was 1917—or was it 1918? André Chapellier, the man, advertised in *Le Carré du Paris* a sincere intention to end his own life. Before a packed house, an audience seated in the galleries of the famous benefactress, Berthe Weill, André replaced a carafe of fresh water (provided for all performances) with a bottle of spirits. To the crowd, his intentions were mysterious as he made this switch with a flourish; he said the alcohol was "for benefit of my nerve." Backstage, he wrapped his loins in long strips of circus-colored canvas—red, yellow, blue and green, slathered his new muscles with a thin polish of lard and then, with four bounds, mounted the stage. As he warmed up the crowd in a pre-suicide *recit,* which was a rant, really, he paced as anxious as an animal in a trap. He covered it all. The important topics. Death, life, misery, happiness.

He then did what they all came to see, did what he'd advertised. Two women fainted, perhaps because he'd extracted his genitalia from the brightly colored bands, lifted and placed his testicles upon the table like two ripe tangerines? And as he stood with his balls (as exotic as fruits waiting for a moist mouth) propped on the slab, he held a gun to his head, pulled the trigger and the crowd gasped. But the firearm only clicked—he'd never loaded the damn thing. The chamber had been empty all along. The audience sighed, and then applauded wildly, but, instead of taking a bow, André tossed the pistol to the floor and glowered.

"Shame on all of you! Death is not an entertainment!" He stared at the crowd, contempt wrinkling his eyebrows, until they all grew silent, contrition washing over the hush. Oh, the joke was on this bourgeoisie group, but they had not known it! And André could not help himself. He chuckled at the dour, pale faces of the shocked group, then broke the pall with a hearty laugh, deep and joyful. The place erupted with merriment and horror, as this new sensation in the art world, this muscular man, stood right there on that stage and proceeded to massage his penis, urinating in a high arc onto the throng until he finally gained a certain hardness and lost his stream. After that, André Chapellier was barred from all public events. At least that year, whichever year it was.

For more than three decades, he was many men and a woman. Thirty men, not one. A bulky man, a wiry man, a person short and tall. André Chapellier was a cunning fellow, sharp blade, a magician with all manner of disguises; he could devise a new appearance for any new name or job. His malleable face, even with the glass eye and warped nose he'd earned through hard living, could be sculpted with a little putty, painted and changed with some dark rouge, if he so desired. He knew all the chameleon tricks. Hair pieces of various lengths and colors; cotton muslin stuffed in cheeks and up the nose; strange round or square eyeglasses to push out his ears or magnify his eyes to the size of salad plates; hats—small or large, round or peaked—depending upon the profession he was faking; baggy or tight clothes for a birdlike or bovine frame. Yes, André was an artist at masking his real appearance, even to those he loved. The real man, if ever glimpsed, was handsome, dashing even, some would say. But reality did not matter to a man of André's ilk. Maybe it was the dreams that grew thick and queer inside him.

At various times, this André, this master of disguise, had passed himself off as a pugilist, poet, professor, prospector; made himself into a sailor, critic, editor, chauffeur; become an orange picker, female can-can dancer, painter and whore; learned the trades of butcher and lumberjack;

and gained the reputation of dandy, forger, cardsharper, or thief. To all, he was the toast of more than two continents, a lady-lover and a man-lover, too. André Chapellier was everything and nothing. Dada.

And then, one day, *Poof!* Like a rabbit down a hole, he'd vanished from Cuba in 1919. No corpse, no note. Only one witness. *They all said, Maybe he's drowned on the high seas or reinvented himself in some faraway land.* The Parisian and New York *avant-garde* knew he'd return. *Perhaps he's taken up the language of some new lover,* they whispered and laughed, as they fucked in their bright-shuttered boarding houses and sipped bootleg absinthe in out-of-the-way cafés, their illegal drinks glowing green like fireflies.

The pectorals of their lost André, the boxer who'd departed, had measured more than forty-two inches around. The ghost of André, the absurd, outrageous poet, haunted the group of Dada. One day he'd been *un fripon,* the next, a chic host wearing a shawl-collared smoking jacket and an evening fez with a dangling, silky tassel that swished about his forehead. He was a contradiction. Just a few years before, in protest of the war that waged in France, the boxer, the fighter, had scoffed at the thousands of tired soldiers and thumbed his way back to Switzerland.

His minor-poet wife, Olivia, of the long nose, tall legs, and rope pearls, the necklace so extensive it trailed like a wedding train behind her, this woman he'd married on a whim just so she'd wrap those legs and pearls around him, well, now, she, too, assented to public opinion, believed, like everyone else, that the missing André had sailed away on some mysterious excursion. (The rumors—but they were true!—were rampant. So many good-natured souls told the suffering wife of her missing husband's three mistresses, and so-called friends did nothing to quiet talk about André's male lovers.) The vulturous crowd all concurred; of course he'd return—André would surely glide back into view. Yes, yes, of course, he *had* to come back to them. Didn't he?

BOXER STATUE

Beneath my puffing lids, I trance and toss
Titleholder eyeballs
From ear to ear only after
I inspect a crowd
Collected almost by happenstance.
Dock workers and doorkeepers and magistrates
And a few starlings, too.
Oh, but in the motley place,
There is the man there on the mat
Who, at first limpid word,
At first laughter of his flesh, is
Foolishness. Ha!
I am torn asunder, bruised.
He exposes himself
And I recall the time I bent up
For the evening beside my medicine ball.

A child-man in love with rubber.
An omnivore.
In the company of this burnished statue whom
I savor and purr with my ocean eyes,
I venerate his palm like a sacred bowl.
But his abdominal mile is my
Favorite attraction.

—Attributed to André Chapellier, *The*
Lost Journals, 1918

As for André (or whatever he liked to call himself at any given moment), he could only hope that his name, or any of his names for that matter—Andy Cabe, Jean Paul LaFleur, Jeb Calder, Sebastian Carter—were still spoken. The power of words—and the lack of them lately—descended upon him in this dreaded silence. All this oblivion made him hope for some remnant notoriety, some vestige of commemoration or reverence that he'd received not long ago, only a few continents away. But, oh, he could so easily obliterate himself anywhere as well. In Europe and in New York, he'd finally run out of things to make them talk. Dadaism was nothing without its scandals.

Most mornings he awoke to ringing quiet here. Just as he had this morning. The dead air of the Cuban coast—it was deafening. He squinted at the bright sunlight streaming in from a curtainless porthole, first focused (with his good eye) on the new hairpiece draped like a marmot atop his clothes. And sitting beside the rodent-looking toupee, his fake mustache curled into an apostrophe, flopped about in the humid breeze. When he stood, his feet did not recognize the strange floorboards, and, in the galley, cool, watery light flowed over his hands.

He'd stolen this boat in Texas. He was now docked somewhere along the coast. His Spanish wasn't good—not yet. It would take him another week or two to climb inside the language, to gain the accent and fluency of a native. Then he'd know exactly where he was. His location? He couldn't get a straight answer from the locals. They did not trust strangers. He knew he had to be close to Havana. Maybe. But who needed a map or compass anyway? Words were the way to find what he needed—that was his credo lately.

It was too hot already, perhaps it was not such a good morning to write. He couldn't find a damn thing to write about, anyway. No more memoirs, no more stories about someone he wasn't. That last fraud was not successful. For a while, he'd had everyone believing he was Oscar Wilde's nephew. It was Olivia who'd discovered his lie. And the exposure was unbearable. When he left her, his wife's cackling laughter bombarded him, yet her disdain was still not enough to push him away; contempt was his line of work, after all. No, something far worse prompted his departure. It was the mewling baby. He never wanted to see it again.

With nothing else to do on the boat, no writing he could conjure, he would get away from the silence of water and head into town. A big breakfast at the good Señora's was in order. A meal of rough tortillas and bright yellow eggs. After he found his mirror and placed the brown hairpiece on his head (his own pate was blond and centimeters short), he stuffed a little cotton batting into his cheeks for fake jowls, then headed to town, for disguises were all he had left.

On the walk, the road was dusty. A pink glint of quartz sparkled in the dirt as he kicked it. It was the shiny dust that distracted him, the fantastical designs moting mid-air. He kept walking, not looking where he went, and, so, the minor destruction happened by accident—André tore into a spider web that spanned the width of the road. As he pulled the silken strings from his face, he stopped and gazed with wonder as the arachnid spun at a furious pace, as he repaired André's hapless damage. The hole was the size of a man. With the web finally fixed, after at least half an hour, the spider returned to his work, weaving a huge filament around the chrysalis of a butterfly. But André had stopped watching. No, he was far away, remembering, dreaming.

In this dream, André, it all surrounds you! Take a deep breath and smell this strange, foreign land, this New World. Take a whiff of apple pies in ovens, frankfurters steaming in black cauldrons, lime dusting street gutters; stale beer on saloon steps. Sniff at the fresh newspapers, the ink still wet; breathe in the stink of horseshit as it steams in piles on the road; inhale the sweetness of fruit ripening on windowsills.

Look at New York! Look around you—at the old negro fishmonger squatting to feed a some tomcats raw halibut; at the tinker struggling with his cacophonous handcart of candlesticks, pie pans, doorknobs, trowels, cookie tins, copper kettles, forks, horseshoes, clasp knives, and screws; at the bakers' wives tied up in yellow head kerchiefs and stained aprons; at the hotel bellboys donning black tails; at the Navy shipmen on shore leave; at the vegetable lady, hands knobbed as roots, hawking her bushels of collards and beets; at the lean shoeshine man veiled in a nimbus of pipe smoke, thin rivulets of saddle soap dribbling down his pants.

Prick up your ears to the old Jews, hats pulled low over their ear curls, pushing trousers and diamonds to passersby; to the little boys with black fingers who yell about yesterday's news from the sidewalk corners; to the plump whores arguing and the young businessmen tabulating; to the newfangled Model T's toot-toot-tooting; to the infant's yowl and the traffic cop's whistle and the multitude of silver bracelets jangling on the wrists of some immigrant woman—a gypsy, no doubt. This melting pot, this stew, this New York. This place where everything is possible. At least that is what you think.

Now, make your way inside the exhibition tent where the stench is sickening: mildewed canvas, unwashed men who've labored long through the day, liquor, old beer and older piss.

"I'd like to introduce myself as the undisputed heavyweight champion of France. *Je suis un peindre* André

Chapellier." Your voice booms out over the bleachers, the French accent coughed out like phlegm. The crowd hurls whatever they can: cigarette butts, bottles, tobacco that's spit with great accuracy. Someone even tosses a boot that hits you on the head. But you don't mind. You prance your finely honed body around the ring as the attendants sweep the rubbish away.

You've practiced this move and that, watched yourself in the mirror for hours. Your fighter's body is the epitome of art, after all. Or the absence of it. In this ring, you know you'll get beaten, even bloody, but *mérde,* you've conned your way into this bout, you're going to follow through. When else will you ever get the chance to spar with the former Heavyweight Champion of the World, Johnny Parker, the Nubian Prince, all purple-black and gleaming in the opposite corner?

After the bell at round one, André didn't remember anything, really, except he knew to take his blows. And when Johnny delivered the last counter jab, followed by a quick, deadly uppercut, when the big boxer sliced open André's chin like a filet, the French poet fell, then sputtered his molar onto the mat. André was smart; he knew to stay down until he heard the word "ten." With that last number, Johnny Parker, the man who'd been the fierce boxer just moments before, came from his corner to offer assistance, to shake hands. He reached down, lifted André to his feet amidst all the hoots. The mob's jeers went to both corners:

"Go home Frenchie!"

"Fucking spade!"

Johnny smiled.

"Whadaya say? Get a drink?" he asked, piffing sweat from the sides of his mouth, ducking epithets, debris thrown into the ring. He grabbed André's shoulder and pushed him to safety. "Move." At that moment, André knew he had a friend.

The air was ripe in the bar. Easy women, ladies of the night who wore cheap perfume, sat on every other stool. This was André's kind of place. In obscurity, he could rub his palm up a whore's warm thigh as he twiddled under her skirt. He and Johnny drank and laughed until late. And with no prompting, at the end of the night, Johnny, the immense boxer, ran an unexpected, tender finger down André's cheek, then sniffed and leaned over to breathe in the Frenchman's scent. André shivered. He forgot all about that prostitute on his knee.

10 *juin* 1917

Dearest Michel,

C'est vrai—the postmark—New York! I'm here at last! What a glorious, uncivilised place. It suits me to no end! I've compiled this primer for you bastards who want to follow to the New World. Only English, write to me only in English. It's the only way to learn. Love to the ladies.

Yours,

André

P.S. This primer is for the benefit of you foreigners. Here are some tips on how you can become the most perfect of American gentlemen:

- Be a splash or two taller than the cop on the corner.
- Scruff will not do! Shave yourself to a soft boy's fleece. Do it to a fault, morning and evening.
- Part your hair. Middle, side, it doesn't matter, just make sure you grease it with some perfumed nonsense. Make the line across your head very crooked.
- Chew on something all the time—tobacco, gum, or even remnants from last night's supper.
- Like chewing, spit all the time, and at most inappropriate moments—on your host's carpet in the parlor, at the theater with its slick lobby floors.
- Pick your nose, dig deep with your fingers. Skill at flicking is important.
- With knees high and fly open, dance the waltz or reel or even a jig.
- Let your money jingle loose in your pockets as you walk down the street, preferably with a wide gait.

- Carouse in bars, drinking nothing but cheap beer piled high with a thick head. Let the foam ferment on your upper lip the rest of the day.
- Loathe women, even your mother.
- With respect to your wardrobe, button-boots and detachable collars are requisite with ill-fitting clothes.
- All haberdashery and suits must be two sizes too big or small.
- Outdated styles are most apt if you are twenty years old or fifty.
- Try to look like your grandfather.
- Wear wool in summer, linen in winter.
- Spats are keen, especially if you want to look like a boxer. Everyone does.
- Bowlers and felt hats are very becoming, even for non-bankers.
- Straw boaters are wonderful in blizzards.
- And always, always, keep your hat on your head, even in church.
- Respect and generosity are not as important as cheek. Remember rudeness reigns. Never hold the door for a lady or proffer a light.
- And never, ever thank anyone. Especially if they have given you something—a cigarette, a steady elbow on muddy terrain. Appreciation is extraneous. You are American, you have more important things to do!

Now, this is how you look and act just like an American!

—letter from André Chapellier, to his friend, Michel Brisebois, printed in *L'Echo des Sports*, 26 *novembre* 1917

Olivia, she is America. Olivia, she flutters at Johnny, with his arm laced around my elbow. Olivia, I forget my infatuation with the boxer. Olivia, across the salon, the big hat a black swan upon her head. Olivia, sauntering forward, sucking the tip of her forefinger like a child. Olivia, the expensive paintings, the heavy furniture, the Buhl cabinets and inlaid dressers, the bewitched ottoman, the satin into velvet, the kneeling, the soft knit braid of hair untwining onto the penthouse floor, the pearls a lasso. Olivia, the harmony of voice and movement, the pointy bone of her clavicle, the blue freckle on her left buttock. Olivia, her sheer white dress, the small, sweet, fragrant freesia bouquet. Olivia, the signature, the calligraphic poet's hand, the register: *New York State, November 7, 1918, Olivia Chapellier, wife, André Chapellier, husband.*

—Attributed to André Chapellier,
The Lost Journals, 1918

Breakfast, and the Cuban señora was cranky. He sat at the crumb-covered table and ate a heaping plate of tortillas, not really tasting the paper-thin crusts, not really chewing, even. At the block, the old woman stood quartering birds for lunch, tossing innards to the roving dogs out in the courtyard. She pitched some skin through the door to a small mutt and then shuffled over to the table, propped one hand on her shelf of a hip.

"*¡Aquí tienes!*" She slid a glass of mountain coffee with a shot of cane liquor in front of him, took his empty plate. The enormous kitchen, with the whispers of the fire and the fecund chickens sleeping on their perches—poised to lay more eggs, he was sure—breathed in calculated, living rhythms. He swallowed down the last tortilla, but drank the rest of his mug in slow sips. He was thinking just as slowly, did not take his eyes off the old woman who was eviscerating birds at the stove. In spite of her age, she wasn't in bad shape. Long legs. Like Olivia.

He remembered the letter. It had stated it all plainly enough. Olivia wanted to see him, wanted to meet him on neutral ground somewhere south of border. She would be in Buenos Aires waiting. The baby would be with her. He could not stand the thought. The slim envelope had come in the general post, when he'd been holed up in some small town in Texas. The work had been hard on the ranch: cutting the balls off bulls, reinforcing fence lines with barbed wire rolled in wheels big as buildings. His wife had found him easily enough. He'd left a forwarding address on the foyer table before he clicked the door shut.

In the letter, Olivia implored him. She wanted him back. Her scratchy writing gave her away. It was desperate—the desperation of a woman with a mouth to feed. Sickening. She even called him *mon chou*. And he couldn't help himself, really. Pure instinct compelled him toward meeting her. He couldn't forgive himself for his own weakness. But he pushed through his disgust, pushed to the coast, where he found a small sloop, something perfect to sail the Gulf and the Caribbean. He stole it.

And as he sailed the sea, with the vast emptiness around him, he found all his needs, even his wants, dissipate. There was no need for Olivia out there on the waves. Life was all about the cutting of the bow, the brisk water and stiff breezes and briny air and the fight against moisture, a wetness that would inevitably rust and rot everything. And now, here he sat at breakfast in Cuba. Dreaming his life. Without certainty, without words, without acclaim, with old señoras and fertile hens and hungry dogs, with nothingness and heat all around him.

> *Never watch from the audience; dream your life*
> *as if you're always on stage.*
> *(André Chapellier, Des Paroles, 1916)*

Before he knew when he was dreaming and when he was awake, before all that, he'd been so far from the person he was now. Years and continents ago. But he always hearkened back to that same immutable dream of childhood. Lush spring fields filled with winter wheat. Sticks and branches crackling under his small weight. Cotton trousers. The soft hand of his grandmother. Collecting wood for the stove. It was all an endless process. But there was a reward. The green twigs would blaze with a bright flame, all sweet and snapping. And fleeting. It was the burning he loved more than the collecting.

"Grand-Maman, I am tired. Can we go inside now?" In the dream, the old woman's response frightened him every time.

"Now, little man, you've been very bad. You'll never go home. *Jamais plus."* Always the same, this dream in his sleep.

And then, as a young man in Switzerland, the dreams took him while he was awake. At his parent's home, he converted the attic into his own room, its slanted walls pressing down. He'd plastered drawings over the fading red and gold rose wallpaper, a pale landscape of wispy petals spaced far apart in repeated patterns. He tacked up all his recent sketches of the view. There were now no images he did not own, except what existed outside his window.

Words were not a part of his world. Not yet, not for a long time. From his bed, he could view the terrain outside, out past a windowsill inhabited by flowerpots and all the way up to the Alps, but never beyond. He wondered about the sea in this landlocked place. And, despite a sometimes rare and intense summer heat, he insisted on wearing the handmade flannel dressing gown that he found in a discarded trunk of clothes. He imagined that it had belonged to some great English-speaking ancestor, a painter, perhaps, or a writer, maybe Constable or Byron or William Wordsworth or Wilde. The faded collar of Queen Anne's lace fastened snugly at his chin with a small wine-colored ribbon, which he tied in a sad bow. The same torn lace hung in ivory trails from each wrist.

He'd retreated to his parent's home shortly after he'd stopped speaking. The move wasn't really his choice. A month after he cloistered himself in his dormitory, his mother, fearing gossip, arrived at university to retrieve him. Without his own words, with only silence as his protest, he was quickly transported home. His mother, always an uncomfortable, awkward woman, never exactly cruel, never exactly kind, professed that she felt no trauma about her son's sudden strangeness. Still, at the end, everyone discerned it was the boy's silence that pressed her swiftly into heaven.

After his mother's sudden death, the young man took his meals in the solitude of his attic. No one ever knew why he gave up the world of language, and, gradually, the people around him even ceased to address him. He rarely left the house. Not that anyone noticed, anyway.

Following breakfast, in town, André purchased two smoked fish and a loaf of flat bread for his dinner, which the Señora carefully placed into a basket pack, cool and dark like a creel. He wished he'd worn something on his feet. That morning on the boat, he hadn't found his shoes under the bunk or on deck or in the galley, so he'd walked into town barefoot, knowing how the gritty road would feel beneath exposed feet, how it might tear at the skin. Now he wished he might have fought that folly. His feet stung from so many little cuts.

It was coming up on early afternoon; he slipped down the long alley past the melon sellers, and no one noticed him. He'd made himself invisible with the concealing outfit of a fellow peasant; no one would have the refined eyes to spot the fine weave of his linen shirt, his only shirt. They were ignorant people here in this land, after all.

And then he spied someone, as he was congratulating himself on an escape from the inevitable *"Buenos dias, Señor"* of pushy vendors. A person he recognized, right there on the road outside of town. It was a man from his world, yes, yes, yes, it *was* someone, one of the many he'd left behind! He squinted to make out the face. He had to be sure. Yes, clear as the sky above him, it was none other than the boxer; it was Johnny Parker, his good friend, riding right past in the town's hired carriage!

Panic. How would he explain himself? André was no one and nothing now. He slumped behind his disguise, and Johnny drove the horses by. And then André noticed the colorful posters all up and down the lane, announcements for a local affair. He focused his good eye, lamped on a rendering of Johnny shadowboxing in the loose handbills that fluttered about the road. Yes, there was Johnny drawn in caricature, a funny, menacing pose, his head huge, his body a bulk of muscles all out of proportion. The notices, pink and orange, like holiday flags, were tacked to all the telegraph poles, pasted on every door of every house in town. They gave the place a festive air. He couldn't understand the meaning of all the Spanish words that advertised the event, but he knew Johnny must have a fight with someone in this godforsaken place. Why here? And André didn't even know exactly where "here" was.

As Johnny had passed, André hid behind a yucca plant; he still watched, concealed in the foliage, as Johnny's horses clipped their way to the top of the sloping hill toward a large, stucco hacienda. Johnny snapped the reins as he continued up the road. Still in plain view, the carriage kept a fast pace along the whole, low, sweeping vista. Just this morning, he had overheard the baker gossiping with Señora about the strange visitors, a couple, *un negro señor* and *una muy bonita señorita* leasing the large *buena casa*. As Johnny halted the carriage to a stop, André could make out the boxer's figure. It was small, like a child's toy from that distance, but still visible in the bright, cloudless air.

André walked along, followed the carriage's trail of dust; where he now strode, a fine powder, like smoke, still hung to the air minutes after the rig had traveled there. He ran, faster, sprinted alongside the lonely route, faster, faster, heaving in the dirty air, hacking from it, but he pushed on, even as his breakfast of eggs and tortillas made their way up into his throat. He could not get sick, not now. He snapped his tongue against the roof of his mouth and dropped his pack with dinner and kept moving. He had to get to the big house, had to see Johnny. André was sure he could explain his own predicament, the obscurity, the disappearance. But why had Johnny decided to fight here? Who would he fight, the Cuban champion? Perhaps André could see him train, could get back into the circuit. Oh, the possibilities! And had Johnny brought Olivia, the whore, with him?

André gained momentum, and his heart hooked to his ribs, his body ached up the rise with effort, the parrots screeching and squawking all the while from the sparse jungle: *Eeeh-ak, eeeh-eeeh, eeeh-eeeh!,* and, in moments, he mounted a stickled grade and moved past the flat sugarcane steppes that greened up the hill. He slipped through a tract of waist-high vegetation, spikes dancing in gusts from the ocean, pointing this way and that. And when he arrived at the big residence, he was breathless with exhaustion and exhilaration, but he kept going. He dodged well past Johnny's carriage parked on the front gravel drive. The horses still waited there, harnessed and thirsty for water; their heads glistened and bobbled in the noonday heat.

Just like the horses, André dripped in a bare liquid way. He crept to the side of the drive. He was breathing a little more slowly now. Calming. And when he felt a sharpness below his knees, he looked down to find that his feet were bleeding from the rough rocks he'd run over, the rocks he hadn't even noticed in his urgency. Small stones and dirt from the road had punctured the skin, and the blood was now dowsed and bandaged with a sticky paste of pink-brown dust. He crouched, skirted low. His feet were burning, but at least their coating of dirt would not leave bloody red tracks for anyone to see. He crawled on his haunches along the edge of a ravine, and then hid in some undergrowth below the stone balcony at the back of the house. First, he had to be sure that Olivia was not here, that she had not traveled with Johnny. Then he had to concoct a good story, one that would get him back in Johnny's good graces. His old boxer friend would be happy to see him, but only if Olivia had not made the trip.

As he lay close to the earth, inside the encroaching jungle, in the thick plants, his heart finally gave way to the quiet. He burrowed his face close to the moist soil, caught the scent of his own fluorescence. André hid there in it, in the earth's fecundity, with his ear to the dirt, the beetles and bugs deep down, digging and crunching, going about their business of living. His eyes flittered, almost closed.

But then, a thunderclap. He jolted upright. And it all fell open. Through the large house's open windows, its gaping doors, it was Olivia's voice that found him. It reached to him out there, hit him like an open-handed slap. She was calming the baby. The child that was not his. It was Johnny she'd always wanted, and, now, she'd finally succeeded in her quest: her small son, the child, was a tiny, diluted version of the famous boxer.

Though André could not make out the words of the woman's distant, precious-sounding baby talk, his wife's raspy, dark tones could not be mistaken, even out there amidst the thick trees and bizzing bugs. He brushed his face, as if to swat at flies, but it was Olivia, her voice, he wanted to push away. Surely, she and Johnny would see him somewhere in town. But only if he stayed. He could leave. His disguises were useless on both of them. They'd witnessed his fun tricks at the wedding, when Johnny had come along to City Hall out of amusement. André had put a good face together for them, happy, jovial, jowls and a moustache. He'd suspected the truth about Johnny and Olivia, even then.

But the truth of it all did not matter now, as André hid under the house in the swelter of early afternoon and felt a rush of unearthed tenderness, an excavated aching traveling the distance, as he peered through the sweet-smelling orange orchids and choking vines. He had a moment of recognition, a moment of stillness, a revisitation, and it all came back. He had loved them both that much.

"*Señor? Señor? Señor?*" A child no more than five, a tiny dirt urchin, had stolen up from behind him in the tangled woods and now tugged at his sleeve. A boy. The caretaker's son, no doubt. Dark, shirtless, this boy. He would reveal André. What would they think of André, a supposed celebrity, lurking like a dog in the bushes outside the hacienda?

"Shhhh." André implored and smiled, then motioned for the boy to sit, to quiet down. He even held up his hands in surrender, adopted a modest expression, one of defeat. Of course, André thought, if this silly boy knew his place, he would understand that a grown man could lie in the brush anywhere he pleased. But the child was suspicious and would not have it. His curiosity would not allow André his hiding place. There was no mollifying the boy.

"*Señor? Señor? ¿Por qué aquí? Yo sé por qué.*" There was a pause, as the boy pondered, then frowned and pointed. And the yelling began.

"*Aquí, aquí, aquí!*"

André thought the stupid boy would ruin everything; he was making a scene. This stupid, stupid boy. André acted then, he did not think. He pulled the brat down, clamped a large hand over the his filthy little mouth, a mouth whose breath was sour with hunger, and the boy struggled, he scratched and kicked, and the smell of crushed leaves was all around them, the freshness, the sharp odor of ruin, and the boy whelped and bit at his captor's fingers, the blood trickling down André's wrists, but André could not let go and held tight as the little hellion fought, *no, no, no,* André could not be seen, *no,* Olivia and Johnny must not see or find him like this, hiding, in ruin, *the shame, the shame,* the child would not stop his fight, he fought and fought, and André would not lighten his grip, he fought, too, he would not lose, he could not let them find him here like this, and it only took moments, a minute, no, two, of pinching the boy's mouth and nose, of hearing him kick at the fat, creeping plants, the crackle of stems under his small feet no louder than the sound of raindrops in a deep forest, and then with one last jolt, the child wilted in his arms. No more sound, no more heartbeat. The horror. The child's eyes still open and questioning, but clouding over. André could still hear the echo of the child's quiet, struggling whine, his fast, labored panting. The boy's last breath was stuck in his ears. And then, the outside world came back to him—there was the smell of tobacco smoke from Johnny's pipe trailing out over the house and soaring yelps from puppies far away in a barn somewhere, a high sound like many bells ringing in dissonance.

Olivia stepped onto the balcony. He didn't think she could see him, but maybe she sensed someone was there. Uncanny. She stood there, still as a corbel leaning over the balcony, watched the brush as he and the little lifeless body stooped inside it. He reached up to his scalp. His hairpiece was lost. And he'd swallowed the cotton in his cheeks as he'd struggled. He was exposed. He covered the child, covered him with his own fine linen shirt, and lay there and wished he were dead, too. Oh, what had he done?

His first thoughts of death, they went something like this: He ran with the boys through the barn, made his way into the abandoned churchyard; there, he concealed himself. He crouched down, screened himself behind a tombstone sunk sideways in the moist earth. The grave marker tilted at an angle. The dead owner's name, long since eroded away, he never knew it. The dead man rested without any words to mark him. He could only make out the words "Devoted husband and father" in the soft, crumbling stone and imagined a faceless, nameless man, invisible, lying in wait, deep in the earth. The boy knew well the effort and cost of waiting. He could smell the mortuary nearby. No one in town ever acknowledged that stench, as if the marble walls could cordon off rot. The reek actually comforted him, the decaying flesh and acrid chemicals always reminding him of some oblivion to come. Ever since, his dreams had weighed heavy.

He was sure Olivia had seen him. He knew what he must do. He walked to the water. To the boat. Left Johnny and Olivia there with the dead child at the hacienda. He would never see them again. No more lies, no more silly, inconsequential scribbles. He had felt real life in his hands. He had pushed it away, too. The waves crashed on the beach ahead. The only sound. He followed it, a living sound.

He bent down and slathered the dirt and blood from his feet and hands (some of the crimson trickling away was surely the boy's), and the sea washed over his fingers and toes. With his back to the sea, he stretched his arms out to his sides, dirt and bloodstained palms shoreward, an offering. The waves swept at his feet, pulling him toward the center of the world, gently reminding him to go to the boat, to the dock. He reached the sloop, untied it from its moorings and drifted, sails down and furled, away from the dock and out to sea.

It was too late when he saw Olivia come after him, yelling his name. Her belly, round and waiting for the birth of his child (he knew it was *his* somehow, that it was not Johnny's). Their baby would be fair and blond and kind and smart; yes, she came after him with her stomach full of potential. Her torso jutted and swayed as she waded as far as her hips. She called out to him. But how could she have known that the name she yelled, "André! André!" was nothing, meant nothing, that he no longer knew himself by that name? He would never be that man again.

Now he was escaping more than names or schemes or words or personas or dreams. Oh, what kind of man had he become? The undertow lugged him far. His once-loved boat wrapped around the surf, and, in response, the tide spun its hull with a mighty force. Sweeping, yes, gradually sweeping him deep and far.

The fishing trawler had been out for several days when they found him, his boat long smashed in the currents. The men joked to each other that he was the biggest fish they'd caught that season. Some believed that this water-logged stranger's survival was miraculous. It surely meant hope for their vessel. Others thought he was responsible for the hundreds of grouper they'd found already dead and floating. And for the red seas. They were convinced that there was a curse upon those who found him.

He was dreaming when they discovered him there, swimming among the fish. Warm sea had temporarily washed away his memories. He'd sunk far beneath the surface, surrounded by a school of black grouper, his clean white hair a glistening halo. It was almost funny how he never sensed the fish, his companions, were all dead. Not even as their slithering corpses brushed his arms and legs, coddling him. He only noticed that swimming in seawater was easy, it slid across his skin. He was light, aloft; he'd taken flight. He was a dolphin. Or a ruby-throated bird. It was so easy to ignore the growing heaviness stitching his lungs, filling them. He opened his eyes. There was a shadow up on the surface; he spotted the prow of a trawler. Its gray hull cut a crease through the blue sunlight above. He never saw the nets.

Within seconds, the men pulled him aboard the vessel. They were celebrating Christmas. An old fisherman dressed as Saint Nick, drunk and dirty, was the first to see him. All those aboard the fishing boat had thought the raving drunk was sea-mad as he yelled, *"Una sirena, aquí*

…. Una sirena, muy bonita …. Mira mes amigos, una sirena."
The drunk, alone, reached with scarred hands and pulled
the strange creature aboard, and then set about separating
the sea from its lungs. He slapped at André's chest the way
he'd seen women beat dirt from rugs. Hard and fast.

The sea left André's near-drowned hulking form as
easily as it had entered him. The water sputtered out of
him in dribbles, then gushes. And then, his gaze fixed
upon the drunk's red nose, which, with years of drink,
had exploded into the shape of a wild mushroom. The
man's Santa costume stunk of sweat and chum; the once-
white cuffs were black from handling nets. As the old man
worked to revive André, the dingy ball of his Santa hat
bobbed and bounced. And although André gave no sign
of fear, the man whispered kind, calming Spanish, as if
cooing to a baby. André slept then. The dreams called to
him like sirens from the shore.

He learned Spanish quickly. And, as he learned, his
dreams changed. Sometimes in his dreams, Johnny visited, his voice sharp, accusing. But it was Olivia who was
always there. She spoke English in flat American tones;
sometimes she spoke French, his mother tongue, in halt-
ing patterns. The harsh rise and fall of Olivia's voice would
move closer, then away again, until months seemed to pass
and her words held no meaning other than the click and
murmur of cyclic sounds, a chorus ululating. Sometimes
the rhythms made him remember the day he'd heard her
calling to him from shore, pregnant with his child (who

was most certainly breathing by now), the day he'd seared through the reef and come to this strange fate. And then, he'd wake from this dream with a start, screaming in horror, as his child, toddling toward him, dirty, shirtless, no more than five, asked, *"¿Señor? ¿Señor? … ¿Por qué aquí? Yo sé por qué … Sir? Sir? … Why are you here? I know why … Monsieur? Monsieur? ... Pourquoi ici?"*

Not long after André's rescue, the cook, the drunk, Beto Piñon, a craggled man in his seventies, took André in as his apprentice. The first day, when Beto watched André cut vegetables, he witnessed a miracle. At least André hoped it seemed sensational. And André read Beto's thoughts, mused at his whisperings. Beto was suspicious, but he was kind. *This young man has never been in a kitchen. But this one learns. And fast. Yes, I saved this glorious man, a gentleman, this golden god from the sea. A good man.* He didn't know André had come to understand Spanish so fast, that he understood all the words the drunken man whispered to himself.

André kept to himself, really, kept the poor cook, believing that he and his shipmates had rescued some fair person who'd been adrift for a long, long time. *Ah,* the cook would say clucking his tongue, *this one's too smart. Ah, the sea has taken the world from him. A husk and a brain, that's all he is. This one has no worries but living and dying; he has nothing, no mouths to feed.* As André listened and watched, he surreptitiously picked up every kitchen skill, learned how to spice the foods, how to combine ingredients into delicious feasts.

Cooking was like writing, a process, one ingredient or stanza after another, a careful melding of components like creating villanelles; it was finding all the right adjectives and verbs, the perfect seasonings, faster and quicker, the rhythm always crucial. He stewed the day's catch with some potatoes or rice, lowered the filleted fish into steaming kelp and boiling ocean water, stirred in some herbs from old cans forgotten in the galley stores. All the while, the old cook sat back and watched this fantastical man move like a steamboat at one hundred knots. Beto sipped his cheap sherry and laughed in awe. Finally, André took over the galley, without wanting it. André could master anything or anyone.

In port, when the long winter catch was over and they'd brought in their last huge haul, André gave every man in the crew, all well fed by his very own hands, a hardy clap on the back and a farewell in his now-fluent Spanish, "*Adios, mes compañeros.*" On that very day, he found a Moroccan vessel headed to Southampton. He signed on as cook's helper.

DEMISE

(A poem attributed to André Chapellier, found in an abandoned journal, written in English, 17 January, 1919)

> *While decks pause in the rhythm,*
> *Back and forth, back and forth*
> *And the clouds swirl like twirling ropes,*

I throw into
The Ocean,
An offering to nobody—
A precious little letter.

The letter lost, a precious little body,
The waves drink it up,
And I see its profound figures leap
In the bitter air,
They penetrate
The drowning of water.

And still
This bold boat,
This beautiful turbine-driven vessel,
Whistles. It goes, it goes!
It pushes thunder
Trailing its long white puff,
After a golden vapor.
It dreams, as I do, of oases,
Of ports in the heaven of glass.
And the trouble of my heart calms,
The purity of equality always the sea.

When not in the galley on the Moroccan ship, André would sit on the stacked, coiled ropes along deck. From where he was, he could hear the crew below playing cards, drinking and arguing. Long ago, these men had bored of the sea and sky. They did not care for the deep or for its tiny waves surprised in petticoats of spume.

Indifference of this magnitude baffled André. How could the men float in the slow, undeniable traffic of tide and not taste its cathedral limits of brine, the surge that ran inside them all? Yes, any time his own schedule allowed, he was drugged by the water's lushness, its lullaby downcast to places far beyond reach; every day he watched the shimmer of gold parchment sunsets until they faded into almonds of night, the gulls gathering and shrieking in sails of shadow. These same waves would soon bathe distant islands, places where washerwomen did laundry on the shore. Oh, the majesty! Maybe, if he gazed at the emptiness long enough, at the fluency of whitecaps on the rough, gray surface, he would find some hidden geometry, some map of meaning.

For as long as he could, he'd disguise himself, mask his feelings, but soon he'd return to civilization, though he was not sure how. The dreams, they still haunted him amidst arcades of stars and sleeping fish. He did know, for certain, that he'd come back here in the end, somehow reunite with the fleeting museum of sea for all time. It could only be true happiness to dissolve into something so great and complete. And his death would be his own doing, he would know the right time. But, strange as it was, he felt a true comfort knowing this. It was enough, after all, to accept that all of him, all of his personas, all the horrors, even the ocean itself, would someday disappear into nothingness.

PART III

THE HUM OF CITIES

The city is a fact in nature, like a cave, a run of mackerel or an ant-heap.

> —Lewis Mumford

High mountains are a feeling, but the hum
Of human cities torture.

> —George Gordon, Lord Byron,
> *Childe Harold's Pilgrimage*

If every man would sweep his own doorway, the city would be clean.

> —Old English Proverb

BLUE

Most days, after a long shift, Blue Kurrin had a finished piece. And the paintings started to get good, too, started to show an individual style. He propped them up outside the Laundromat against the glass with a hand-lettered sign—DO YOUR LAUNDRY, GET A PORTRAIT! But business only trickled in. Sure, people would show faint interest after they saw the colorful pictures up close. And most agreed to let him paint their likeness. But they were all reluctant subjects. Corinne was, too. For a month, she'd pulled up in her pickup truck with Oregon plates, carrying her plastic bags of dirty clothes inside on her hip. Blue would catch her looking at the pictures, but she never said a thing. He knew it was only a matter of time; she was only building up nerve to ask.

One day, after Blue had watched Corrine peruse his work for a good thirty minutes, as the dial on the washer inched its way toward the rinse cycle, she came out with her question.

"You really paint portraits?" Her voice was unsure, her eyes darting to all the paintings hung on the wall. "Can you do me?"

So he began his initial sketch of her—all reds and purples, not quite the way she wanted. "No wild colors, please." He only painted what he saw. As he worked and her laundry dried, she made slow conversation. Her mouth twitched a little as she talked, and he thought she was the most exotic person to ever step foot in his Laundromat.

"Drove here from Oregon to see my kids. They live with my ex's parents. Two of 'em. Boys, seven and twelve."

"You don't look old enough to be outta college, let alone have two sons!" He said. She blushed. "Whatcha do in Oregon?"

"Deep sea recovery and exploration. I'm a scuba expert." And he thought then that she smelled like the sea, all briny and moist. That was all he needed for inspiration, to give his rendering some interesting, personal touches. So he painted her in a black wet suit, with a mask on the top of her head like a hat and tanks slung over one shoulder. She posed for him in the Laundromat's orange plastic chair, but, in the painting, he made her stand upon a jutting sea cliff over an angry ocean, then dabbed in some choppy green waves slapping, no, *spraying*, the tall, wet rocks. For that trick, he used his finest, thickest brush.

But when he got to her eyes, when he needed to finesse the details, she ducked her head, just as he was trying to get the color right. Her face flushed. It was an interesting face.

"Look up for me, will you? Yes, lift your chin." He painted her eyes the way he saw them: a deep gray with a bit of green, the color of distant mountains protruding tall from the ocean. He worked on her eyes, perfecting the faraway feeling, until closing time.

For payment, she gave him a coin, a small, different-looking coin. He acted pleased, though he wasn't sure of the significance.

"You wanna go for a drink or something?" Blue asked as he switched off the lights.

"You got anything to drink at home?" They loaded her laundry into the bed of her truck, left his car in the shopping center, and she drove while he held the portrait in his lap, trying not to smudge the still-wet paint.

"About that coin," Corinne said as they turned into his parking lot. "It's an extraordinary nickel. They don't make those buffalo nickels anymore. Could be worth a lot. My father used to collect 'em, now I only got a few left. The last things I got of him," she said, as she patted Blue's pants pocket with the nickel in it. Her touch had a bright current to it. He glanced out the passenger window; Corinne was different now that he wasn't painting her, more sure of herself.

They sat in the kitchen, all neat and moon-blond with its silvery pots and pans on hooks, the navy shutters at the window, the narrow clenched spirals of the braided rug. At the kitchen table, they talked about their lives, how they were between places. Blue sat close to her.

"Yeah, I'm not so sure if I'll head back to Oregon ...." She flipped her sable hair with her fingers, let her voice trail off. He couldn't help but notice her mouth, white teeth, with a crack bleeding down the middle of the lower lip. It danced when she spoke. "You always been an artist?" He nodded yes, not wanting to go into it. He wanted to show her photos of his art from back East, the pack of snapshots buried in the pile of papers, under all the magazines, letters, bills, offers to develop film in twenty-four hours, coupons for delivery pizza. It all sat next to a snow globe on the shelf.

He was nothing now. Had nothing. He couldn't tell her all that. Instead, he reached over and took the sweaty beer from her hand, placed it on the table. It grated across spilled sugar on the tabletop as he slid it away. He kissed her, tasted the ocean on her tongue.

In bed, she was quiet on top of him, responsive yet quiet. They didn't speak, but listened to a Muddy Waters tape blaring in from the kitchen. The guitar bellowed and groaned. It spoke for them. They moved with each other, into one another. And then, her body jolted, it froze altogether. At full stop. She settled like a bag of moist sand on top of Blue, and nothing, not even loud pleading in her ear, would wake her. In the midst of him thrusting, she'd sagged into sudden sleep; he lay there inside her still, his penis bruised-feeling and dense with what lay unfinished. And when he wilted, too, back to his normal state, he finally rolled her off his stomach. He'd heard of people who couldn't control the tide of sleep, but he'd never seen it firsthand, like this, at the height of whatever it was they'd been doing.

Corinne stayed like that all night, in that deep state, on her back, flaccid and breathing slow. He watched her, made sure she was OK, and after he finished what she had started, pulling it out of himself with careful, quiet strokes, he felt a compulsion to draw her while she lay there. Not finding any paper in his desk, he drew her portrait on a paper towel. Her face, the arms, their smoothness, the curve in her belly, the notch where her hips met her stomach. His chest drew tight like hands folding. And after he scribbled the initial anatomy and started on shading in the creases, he realized this was the first time he'd created something outside the Laundromat since he started back to his art.

It began simply enough, almost a year ago in the Atlanta coin-op, as Blue made quick character sketches, renderings of all the interesting faces waiting to return to their lives. Launderers were always bored, always impatient. No one smiled or even talked to each other. That was OK. Blue didn't like the way smiles created certain lines on faces anyway. And, ah, yes, a man sobering up in the morning was a beautiful thing. Blue would dabble in some red, bloodshot eyes with a marker and pencil in soft lines for jowls, a slash for a mouth.

His boss, Mr. Hong, was like an absentee landlord. He trusted Blue, gave him free reign. Days were all ordinary in the Laundromat: Blue passed out change, emptied money from all the machines. And when he mopped up at closing time, he always found stuff someone had left behind—sticks of gum, half-drunk bottles of Scotch, and money, lots of money, with the bills wet from the washers or shredded from the dryers. Why the hell didn't somebody notice when they left a wet dollar bill clinging to the inside of a washer, or why would anybody drive off without their nice shirt?

He noticed and wondered about these small things. He collected the more memorable items, kept them on a shelf at home—a snow globe from Yosemite that leaked thickish fluid when he tipped it, a bright aqua ball of string, a Kewpie doll with the lips worn off. These were just a few sentimental items he could not pitch, even if their owners had forgotten their importance. But the art supplies he'd found—oils, pencils, brushes, easel, all in a box, he kept those at the Laundromat. He wouldn't shelve those. Some stupid student forgot them, never came back for them.

His art in the Laundromat, in a matter of months, went from rusty, quick jots and sketches (fundamentals he remembered from art school) to virtuoso renderings in oil on canvas. They became more elaborate in composition. He spent all his extra money on supplies. He lost weight. The paunch around his middle, once like a life preserver, was replaced with a tautness, a skeletal quickness. He often forgot to go to the barber next door. His hair grew longer, shaggy. Soon, painting consumed all his time at the job. Nights, he stayed extra late to close up; he swept and wiped away all the powder detergents and drips of fabric softener from tables and the tops of washers well after ten p.m.

And with every morning, first thing, he set up his easel behind the red Formica counter, threw a tape of *'Round Midnight* into his boom box, then waited for Charlie Parker's sax to blare out from the speakers. Customers got real moody when they listened to jazz; it made for better portraits than all that happy stuff on the oldies stations. Blue would wait for someone interesting to come in, then start painting. He'd imagine the guy skulking at the folding table was some Russian spy who got fired from the KGB for not making the grade, a spy who lost his way and was now running books for the Russian mob. The guy's flamingo-patterned polyester shirt and all the artificial fibers in his laundry basket only confirmed Blue's wild imaginings. Everyone knew mobsters wore polyester—that was a given. You could tell a lot from a person's laundry. So Blue did this man's Eastern European roots some justice with a Chagall-like portrait, all bright hues and wispy lines.

And the younger launderers who came in with their jars of quarters, who never asked for change, they were discards, too. The particular young woman with her plastic bag of dirty clothes, with the scant skirts and tied tops, thong undies, no socks, her tanned legs and dark hair like an angry cloud torn by the wind—she was definitely from the West Coast, he thought, and he wondered why the hell a cutie like that would move to the South? To follow her dreams? Yeah, sure, Georgia had a lot to offer. Right.

But when he popped Ella Fitzgerald into the boom box and turned up the volume, that little brunette went into her own scat, and he knew he was in the presence of a natural jazz lady. The girl sputtered and spat her words, syncopating with the machines' cycles—suds, wash, rinse, spin, and permanent press, low and high. All the cycles spun to the beat. When she sat down, waiting for her dryers to finish, he improvised with her picture as she had improvised with her voice. For her, lots of scratchy lines and maybe a little cleavage under the wetsuit. Bright green, a little magenta thrown in. That was Corinne.

And as he watched her sleep, now, like a corpse in his bed, he drew her with a fine No. 1 pencil he sharpened with a kitchen knife. He defined her cheek, drew her lips pursed and soft, with a hint of shading to fill them out. And just when he finished up the drawing, a bright, buffy dawn bloomed in the dusty panes, and light jigged through a crack in the teal curtains. It was only when the watery light warmed her face in filtered shades, all sapphire and emerald through the curtains, that Corinne woke up. She opened her eyes and, before anything else, before stretching even, she smiled at him. Her teeth were all silvery as if she were under water.

Blue decided he'd paint her like that later, smiling, in the buff. He'd never painted a smile before. Never really wanted to.

"Oh, look at the time!" she said, glancing at the bedside clock. Blue pulled on his jeans and stood there waiting. He pulled his hair back and crossed his arms over his wide chest.

"Do you mind?" she said, as she swirled her finger, directing him to turn his back, to keep his eyes to himself, then covered her chest with the comforter but left her bottom half exposed. She bent under the bed to find an errant sock, and though she didn't know it, he could see her reflection in the dresser mirror. Over her rear, close to her spine above her sit bone, she had a long, curved scar, as if something jagged had ripped into her, its deep crimson a shock against her otherwise smooth, pale skin. Like a smile. He wondered why he hadn't felt it during sex.

They walked arm in arm out to the parking lot.

"Well, can I reach you?" he asked. "Maybe call or something?"

"I'll see you, maybe at the Laundromat," she said stretching. Then she looked at him, the sides of her mouth quivering. "You know, Blue, this was nothing. And … I don't have a phone." She seemed apologetic or regretful or resolute—he couldn't decide which—as she slid into her truck.

He stood there in his bare feet. His chest tightened again like a fist. And as he held her door handle, he tried to keep her just a moment longer, searching her face.

"Hey, what if I paint you again? You know, like a figure study or something. It would be great and you wouldn't have to pay." It was a harmless question.

"Sorry, I've really got to go," she said, picking at her crackled steering wheel with her nail. She started her engine and took off, the scuba portrait sitting beside her in the front seat like a passenger. After the last glimpse of her taillights, he reached down and yanked an armful of gentians from the parking lot flowerbed; they were the deep emotional color of the ocean beyond the sight of land.

He wondered about Corinne, about her scuba diving. He thought about her plunging into the cold, how she salvaged wreckage from the deep sea, her tanks on, her rubber suit slippery and warm. He went about his business since he last saw her, tried to paint an old lady with a vanload of comforters. But his attempt at painting the van lady turned into a big, scribbling mess. He tried to do a charcoal sketch of the homeless guy rifling through the shopping center Dumpster out back. But the colors just would not come.

And the week wore on. He searched the face of every new launderer coming through the door. It took a few days for it to sink in. Corinne would not be back. And one morning at three, after tossing and turning, wondering what it would've been like to come inside her, he went to the kitchen for a glass of water. On the table, the flowers, the ones he picked when she left, the gentians, were drooping. Their stems bent weakly, the rich petals all furled and closed.

He couldn't stand it a moment longer and stomped back to the bedroom. No, he couldn't sleep in those sheets, with Corinne's salty scent still reeking in them. He shook off his last bit of drowsiness and stripped everything from the bed, stripped her smell away, then splayed on his bare mattress and tried to sleep again. Maybe he'd paint another portrait of Corinne, anyway. He didn't need a model; his memory was good. He could invent a pose, a picture. He turned on his stomach, thought about her scar, about how she might have gotten it. Perhaps she'd caught her back on a nail or sat on a shard of glass in her driveway. No, it was too big for a minor household fumble. Maybe sharks or some other carnivorous animal. A scuba diving accident? Blue rolled over, found her buffalo nickel on his bedside table, its weight heavy in his hand. He thought about the pencil drawing he'd done of her. She'd looked cold, strewn across the sheets like that. All night he lay there, reminiscing, curled up on his bare mattress and pillow, until the alarm clock buzzed.

He got to the Laundromat early. It was nice there in the quiet morning, no machines vibrating or twitching with strangers' clothes. The machines all stood still, in rows, waiting for their first loads. There was a blissful expectancy in that waiting. He kneaded her nickel in his palm, cranked up Etta James on the boom box. And, as the fluorescent lights flickered above him, heating up for the day, he pulled his paints from their box with a new fervor and unfolded the easel. Then he remembered his sheets and the blanket still reeking of Corinne, which he tossed from his duffel bag into a triple loader. He plunked the Buffalo nickel with some quarters into the coin slot of the washer, and turned the knob. And before too long, the washing machine was sloshing away Corinne, in wild waves of onyx and manganese.

Blue watched the cars go by outside in the milky dawn, waited for the first launderer, usually some old man or a tired mother with her kids snoozing in car seats. He hummed to the strains of Etta's wails, and from the back workroom, he brought out all his paintings. There were dozens of canvasses, dozens of nameless strangers, faces of people who'd sat around and waited impatiently for their clothes to dry so they could get back to their lives. They were all flat faces, good faces, faces about which he couldn't care less.

Now, with all the paintings propped on carts and tables and spread about, Blue had himself an impromptu audience. They'd keep watch as he painted a new work. He could see the gulls in this nascent creation already, could hear their cries; he was already gazing at the frost-shattered masses of the precipice Corinne would stand upon, her back to him. She was so precariously close to pitching into the far blue, the cerulean waste of sea. On a palette, he blended his pigments. Some crimson, with a dash of violet and sienna—the deep, jagged hue of a fresh scar on a woman's pale back. Or maybe it was just the shade of a cold, twitching smile.

RED COAT

What else to do but walk? Flat-footed, hands stuffed in my pockets, big red coat, my hood drawn up as if I'm some little girl with a basket in hand who's visiting her grandmother. Sure, I could take the bus, but then I couldn't eat my soup-in-a-cup. Only one pound a day to spend in Edinburgh. One pound a day from the bursar.

This is a street called Lawnmarket. This is a park called Holyrood. That little lad in some tartan kilt smiles a no-tooth gap. He drinks his stout. He is fat-up on stout and no jobs.

This is the way to town. Pavers worn to dirt by local feet, small feet, big feet, tourist feet. All kinds of shoes. Ghillies, bootblack wingtips, Army issues, ballet flats. On these wrinkled, cinched-in streets, I search for work. The light is murky, diluted like tea from a twice-used bag, and everywhere the same word is tossed at me—no. No jobs. They don't even slam doors in my face.

These are the stone steps that crease up from New Town to Old. The groan of some bagpipe down on Princes Street wails for tourists as footfalls still echo around me, louder as I go up, the sound bouncing off the high walls like acrobats.

This is High Street, and I duck into an alley, hear the tattoo of footsteps clattering, sounds aiming toward destinations. Not me, I have nowhere to be. I prop my forehead against a dank brick, the softness of moss a welcome comfort, and above, the crying gulls slice gauntlets, slash through a swag of drooping clouds.

This is where I tuck my red coat around my chapped face. A mist mopes in dampness, washes away the puke piles on the road. Last night's stout has come to these regurgitated loads spewed by young kilts on the dole, all those laddies who spend their last pence in pubs named One Legged Johnny's, MacGregor's, the Old Toad.

This is where I leave Old Town, down to the Upper Meadows, the castle a shadow, a purple smudge in the twilight. I walk through a brown haze of smoke; there is the sharp odor of burning peat. An old craggle man in fingerless gloves jingles change in his dented cup. He begs in brogue, tongue thick with cold, "Cuppa, cuppa?" I have nothing to give. I fold my shame under my collar and watch someone's dog work a bone in the park's high grass. There's a game of soccer, jocular calls and yellow sports socks.

Down the hill, this is me luging on the grass; it quivers, it breathes in the wind, the meadow moves in waves, the scent of brine sharp from the firth below. The sun lowers behind the hills, a slow, unfolding fan of fire. Three magnificent swans glissade across a small pond; a fourth flies in and skids to a spraying stop. They all slide along the surface, orange beaks and snowy esses of long, languid necks. The males begin to bicker, they quibble and bark, poke at one another, vicious.

It is time to go.

This is my hostel, my bunk. I fold my clothes, and, with money from my pawned watch, I pay my prorated rent and air-kiss all the Aussies good-bye. On the late-night train, I ride away south, the city lights skimming past. Darkness swallows the Highlands and, out the window, there's a star-stung sky. My backpack on my knees, I unlace my boots, the soles worn to paper. At last, I shirk off my red coat, wad it, and kick it under my seat.

COSTUME

When her father dropped her off at school that morning, Zelda reminded him again, but he was distracted, shifting in his seat, digging deep in his pants pocket for her lunch money.

"Dad, remember, it's in just a couple hours. It's *this* morning, ten a.m. Sharp. Sit in the front if you can, OK? Hey, Dad? You hear me?"

"Umm-humm, doll, love ya," he answered, his voice trailing off as he switched stations on the radio and pushed past static, and then he revved the engine as she stepped back. He sped off in the old Malibu, not waiting for Zelda to slam her door shut. It swung open as he two-wheeled the corner, and she lost sight of him with the car door still pivoting open.

Backstage, Sister Saint-Pierre helped all the girls with preparations as the minutes ticked down. Zelda slipped on her costume, dabbed at the pink blusher across her cheeks, and blotted some more electric blue eyeshadow over her lids. Sure, her father was nowhere to be seen. Sure. But Dad was always late—for everything. Getting him to show up was a matter of planning and action. It was a matter of survival.

All those weeks leading up to the assembly, she'd taped reminder notes everywhere—"Zelda! Performance! Friday, September 30, 10 am! Don't forget!" She'd magneted notes onto the refrigerator, glommed messages with chewing gum onto the bathroom mirror; she'd even drawn pictures on the boxes of plastic wedding-cake figurines that her father sold. The big cardboard containers littered the cramped living room, but somehow the graffiti livened up the place with all her crayoned smiley faces. She went so far as to put a large sign, poster size, on the big bag of confectioner's sugar that sat in her dad's back seat like a forgotten lumpy child.

Zelda took a deep breath, inhaled the strong aroma of the school gym—sweat and floor cleaner. She smiled at herself in the mirror one last time.

"All right, girls, let's pray." Sister Saint-Pierre, her homeroom 4B teacher, scooted the girls into a circle, and, as Zelda stood holding hands with the others, she wondered if Dad had found a good seat in the audience.

At the Sign of the Cross, they all got to their places. Sister Saint-Pierre caught Zelda's eye and smiled.

Zelda stood with her arms raised behind the musty curtain, poised to move at the first swish. And then, the overhead lights dimmed and there was a deep silence and the red velvet curtains parted.

In the dream of a few minutes, her dance was magic. She jumped and turned, never missed a beat of the tinny music on the old record player. Flash bulbs sparked from the risers. It was otherworldly. Her feet fluttered like an insect's delicate wings, and the music's violins buzzed, too, as she flitted through the flower props on the stage. As the world fell away and her dance became everything; it didn't matter that those crêpe paper flowers weren't real. No, everything was real, more real, and she could actually smell the crush of pansies underfoot. The audience faded away; the bumbling dancers behind her disappeared. She twirled and pranced, swayed and sashayed, until the music died, until the very last clap and her very last curtain call, when she curtsied to wild applause.

After the lights came up, she waited, watched as all the girls' parents came backstage bearing hugs and flowers—some girls even got stuffed animals. She waited. No one noticed. She tiptoed to the edge of the stage and peeked through the crack in the curtain. Kids and teachers filed out the gym like orderly ants. She stood inside the stale-smelling velvet a long while, searching the empty place. Only the janitor was there, folding chairs off the gym floor.

She slowly folded her tights into her big gym bag and hung her tutu in the costume cabinet, and then Sister Saint-Pierre came in and sat down on the bench.

"You coming to class?" she asked.

"Yes, Sister." Zelda tied her saddle shoes in fast, tight double knots.

"I thought you might like this. You looked so beautiful. I took this Polaroid from the front row." The photo was dark, but Zelda could still make out her costume and all the girls dancing behind in the background. It was a good picture, focused at least; it was easy to tell that the costumes had been bright.

She placed her satiny auburn bodice gingerly on another hanger in the cupboard, then smoothed her fingers over the whole ensemble one last time.

She had come to the Sacred Heart Academy just last May, after Mom haddied, at the end of the school year. Not much time to make friends before the summer break. But she hadn't minded the hot months between third and fourth grades: long days of yard play and discovering woods. There were books to read she found in the library, and when it was too quiet, she watched soap operas with their large, talkative families. Her father was home late most nights.

Then fall ruffled the fringes of summer. Fourth grade had different rules altogether. She picked a desk at the back of every classroom, thought of herself as a small animal hiding, waiting for danger to pass. She'd seen squirrels in the crooks of trees hold still for hours; it had worked for them. Outside, at recess, in P.E., or even during tornado or fire drills, she was always in the back. When she sat at the lunch table where the friendless and social outcasts were relegated, it was peaceful, everyone eating in quiet solidarity. All that chewing.

After the assembly performance, in class, all the girls propped their wilted flowers, gifts from their parents, on their desks. Zelda sat at her desk in the back, pretended to read a dictionary. She had the Polaroid, though, a talisman, a precious memento. All day she sneaked glances, slipped it out of her book bag during a filmstrip about King Tutankhamen, slid the picture out from under a book on her desk during math and spelling. Her mind was still on that stage.

After school, she waited with the carpools until the safety patrol were folding their Day-Glo orange belts. She sat on the hard curb, her arms wrapped around her knees. She thought about the time her dad had wrecked the car on his way home from his favorite bar, how he'd missed her first day of fourth grade—"Honey, if you'd a been riding shotgun, I wouldn't a hit that pole." As she sat there, she hardly noticed the butterfly that landed two feet in front of her on the white parking line. But then a second fluttered down and then a third, and she raised her head to see, out of nowhere, hundreds of monarch butterflies flickering through the bushes and trees, with more floating down through the warm, dry sky. Soon, the thin grass darkened with orange-and-black insects. The sky lost its brightness, as if smoke was blowing in from some distant fire. The willow trees trailed with the weight of thousands of the airborne creatures, and the large golden oaks and their fall plumage dimmed.

The soccer team stopped kicking balls on the field below and sprinted up to the parking lot where stragglers were gathering. Mr. Jennings, the soccer coach and science teacher who'd once fed a piglet to a python, yelled, though there was no noise, as if he expected such visual profusion to make a racket. "They must be flying home to Mexico for winter! We must be on their migration route!"

The butterflies perched on Zelda's arms, shoulders, legs. All the kids were exclaiming and moving around too much to be landing pads, but Zelda stood still, like the inside of a box, as the feathery wings tickled her. She closed her eyes, and it was as if hundreds of eyelashes were blinking all over her skin. When she opened her eyes again and squinted, she caught a light dusting at the tip of her nose as a monarch balanced there with its pin legs. The round, black dots on its wings gazed right back at her with unblinking eyes. It lofted away into the thick air.

The wonder spanned the minutes, until her father pulled up in the parking lot. Curtains of monarchs dodged him as he got out of his car, as he pushed his way through butterflies puffing around the schoolyard. Her dad wobbled a little as he reached her. She knew his condition the instant he drove up, the way his car tires squealed to a stop.

"Honey! Got here soon as I could. Let's get going." His breath was like a blowtorch. "Isn't this marrrr-ve-loussss? They're all down the street, too." He swept his hands in an overexaggerated way toward the sky and butterflies, mimicking them by flapping his arms. His tie was loose and cocked to one side. He winked.

Zelda looked up. The butterflies kept coming. She turned and faced the swarming butterflies. They still roosted and shivered on her arms and legs, clinging to her saddle oxfords and shirt collar and cuffs as living attire; she started out slow, twirling in languid figure-eights, careful not to ruffle the fragile beauty that adhered to her, and then she danced her solo from the assembly.

Zelda then remembered the photo in her pocket. The idea came to her from nowhere—like the butterflies. One last glance at the smiling dancer in the picture, and she slowly started her destruction, she ripped the tough Polaroid paper to flakes, tore it in tiny slivers and flung the tatters, hoping they'd fly like the butterflies, however strange and new as they shared the busy insect air. The pieces scattered in the rising wind and whipped across the scrappy grass and parking lot, and the butterflies winnowed and tinged everything a new color.

For a long time, Zelda danced and danced, with no smile on her face, no expression, really, in her new costume of monarchs. She did not know if her father was watching and she did not care.

LIE TO YOURSELF

It's easy to wreck your life. Really. Just lie to yourself. No, that's too easy. To wreck your life, to start out with, you should ignore your bills. Or better yet—oh, yes—make an *effort* to mess things up! Lick stamps with all the wrong outgoing postage and slap them on all your bills with misprinted return labels so your payments won't get to where they're going, so they go to the dead letter office. Nothing gets paid. So, when the phone's cut off and your temp agency can't reach you and the trailer rent comes due and you don't get that paycheck and you're getting kicked out, you'll only have $1.33 in your bank account.

And then you slide. You find yourself in some ramshackle trailer in Alabama snorting lines of blow a foot long. Your boyfriend flips out and smacks you a dislocated jaw, and you crack it back into place, but not before you get the hell out of there, pitching everything you can grab into the back of your Nova. When the car breaks down, you abandon it somewhere on the shoulder of the interstate—you can't afford gas, anyway—and you thumb the rest of the way with your dog.

When you get to where you're going, though you're not sure where that is, you can't afford an apartment yet. And you can't stay at the YWCA—they don't take pets. Bill's your dog. He's a miniature poodle. So you stay with some man you met yesterday at the Laundromat—his clothes were drying, and you and Bill were inside staying warm.

Laundromat guy will be home from his delivery job soon. You hurry to the corner, to the Magic Market. You rush to buy dog food for you and Bill so that you can eat before Laundromat guy gets home. You're ashamed. Alpo's not a great meal, but at least it's protein. So you purchase the dog food with gooey coins you find between the cushions of Laundromat guy's Barcalounger. You eat the Alpo with some crunchy rice you find forgotten in a take-out carton at the back of the guy's refrigerator. And Bill laps up all the extra dog food you can't push down your throat.

You start peeling shrimp at Shoney's and serving burgers in a box, wearing aprons and hairnets and searching under plates for thirty-five-cent tips. You move to a motel, steal sheets from Mexican maids, and spend your last dollars on baloney and Kool-Aid. You never see Bill. He stays in the bathroom.

You find another job. Any job. Nights at your new, shitty cocktail waitress position—no tips and you have to wear short skirts—you sit up with the female bartender. You drink cheap well bourbon while you watch the Olympics on TV. "Let's be somebody!" the bartender shouts. You let her touch you because, hell, the bartender gets all the free booze you both want. Her girlfriend has left her, cut off all her shirts at the elbows, and changed the locks, so you both have to pry open a window at her place whenever you want in or out. The bartender talks on and on about going back to school or learning to fix things like appliances. You know she never will. Like you, she'll just sit around and talk about it. But you don't say anything. You sit on the farthest stool you can find and watch her pour another round.

Then the bartender moves away without any note. She's just gone and you eat Velveeta on toast for two weeks and think about forgiveness. But Bill gets his dog food. He always does.

You find a job at a nursing home for six bucks an hour. You wear pink scrubs and tennis shoes, and you don't have to swish your ass around customers anymore. And then you notice the hierarchy. Old folks with memories are the nicest, while the ones with nothing upstairs, they treat you as if you don't belong on this Earth. But everyone tolerates you when they want something, when you serve their breakfasts, change their bed linens and empty brown piss from their bedpans.

You wander the antiseptic-scented halls and are invisible in your cheerful uniform. No one will ever know, before you got fat on cheap, fast food, that there was a time in your life you turned heads on the street; that your painting teacher at community college thought you had real talent and even invited you to one of her fancy cocktail parties where you drank expensive wine with a cork and stood under a twinkling chandelier discussing theory with bald men wearing tweed; that you actually sold three prints once and won a fellowship to a famous design school. But you never followed through. In those days, you dreamed of a life filled with hand-holding and tall trees and sloping, green lawns, but that was before you ended up here at the nursing home, where you try not to gag as you chuck some old lady's runny shit down the toilet.

So, you've almost completely wrecked your life. You live in a one-room basement apartment downtown. And lately, Bill looks skinny and scared, shivering when you return home every night from your shift. And then a girl in the complex gets raped. And another. You move out in a hurry, and the landlord keeps your deposit—five hundred bucks. It'll take you another two years to save that much.

You are back at the motel. You wake at three-thirty a.m., confused, not sure where you are for a few moments. It's because you don't belong here. This can't be your life. You are an imposter. You sleep on top of the covers, the bed half made, your socks on, the TV blaring at full volume. Bill's scuffling and whining in his nightmares under the bed. And, as you try to fall back asleep, an infomercial drones on and on about ab machines. Some blond model smiles into the camera; her life is perfect. You sigh and cradle your pillow, push your face into its cold side and whisper, "I love you," just to hear the words.

IT'S NOT YOUR HAT

Your first week back from break, you attend French 201. You hate the French and their abstract words, but you need the credits to graduate. You've put off this class until your last semester. It lasts for hours. Outside during a break for coffee and cigarettes, everyone stomps around on the arctic sidewalk, blows smoke and vapored air. A little bitch with wiry hair approaches you. She points at your open bag, where a hat peeks out like a scared animal.

"That's my hat."

"No, it's mine." You jerk at your bag's loose flap, pull it over the *chapeau*. "It's *mine*." You stand taller. You aren't cold anymore. She persists.

"I lost it yesterday."

"Sorry." You shrug and shift, gazing at the snowy quad.

"That's my hat." Your accuser's black hair frizzes in a calamitous scribble—she really does need the hat more than you do.

"No, it's mine," you echo and turn your back. The words feel wrong rolling off your tongue. But it's January Upstate; it's finders, keepers. You hear hard breathing and turn back around to find she hasn't budged; her hands are fisted in her mittens. You lie again, insistent: "It's *mine*."

But the hat isn't yours. You found it abandoned yesterday on the worn oak benches outside the English Department. You admired the black wool, its flowered cotton lining sewn with crude fever stitches. You looked around, then pulled it low over your forehead and tromped home in the snow, glad you had something new, something warm.

"Let me see," she shrills. People stare as bitchy, antennae-haired girl's voice pitches. "Let me see!" She grabs at your closed bag, but you catch her dark eyes, square her gaze, and pretend you're strong. She stops her advance and now uses reason, her voice squeaking with rage. "I *saw* the lining. A friend did *that*."

"No, this is my work. I've sewn all my life." One lie. One truth. You walk out of arm's reach, pull out the hat, plop it on your head. Break's over.

The hat's hot in the stuffy room. You're ashamed, cornered, but you keep up the front. The gray professor rambles on in French about declensions and past pluperfect. *Parlez vous* shit?

The girl sends out glaring death rays from behind you. She sighs meanly. You wish you'd said you'd found it. You wished you hadn't lied. You don't know why you did.

You go shopping after class. A bell trills, incandescence embraces you as you enter the shop, and the East Indian lady, wrapped in her bright scarves and the scent of curry or something that smells like a balmy night, looks up and, as always, says something kind.

"Good to see you today."

In the back, you fold a Tree of Life tapestry into your bag—the pattern's similar to the hat's lining.

At home, you cut a large square from the stolen textile, center on a perching turquoise bird. You rip out the girl's lining and its crude, thick thread, sew the hat with new, silken stitches, glossy and feather thin.

The next day, you drop the French class. You seldom step foot on campus for fear of running into the girl. You don't graduate for another year. You hide the transformed hat in your bottom bureau drawer where it will sit for years. Funny, but you cannot throw it out.

Let Go

It was three a.m. at the Krispy Kreme. I noticed her skin first. Lustrous and dark, like the coffee I was waiting to order. Before I started my hormone therapy, it had taken me at least two shaves and three layers of pancake to get skin that looked that smooth! So, that night, I stood there in line, and I checked the lady out, up and down, the way a good queen sums up the competition. Nothing else had fared as well as her glossy cheeks; her arms were rough and dry. When I looked closer, as I edged up to the counter, I saw her arms close. Track marks pocked the length of them. The poor thing had no fashion sense, either—she was stuffed into a tight magenta jumpsuit and was all portly like an uncooked sausage. It was when she moved that she had real problems. The woman jerked around like a puppet dragged through water. And she stood there, legs splayed, arms waving, and spoke in alternating tones, gibberish, mainly—bellowed questions and whispered cursing. Goddammit, all I wanted was some coffee.

So I stood close behind her, and magenta lady reordered and recounted her cash for the fifth time, ordering, then retracting, then ordering again. The clerk stood with one hand on her hip, the other on the cash register, staring into space, impatient, irritated. I needed my goddamn cup of coffee.

Some cute straight guy, who'd been pacing the fluorescent-bright restaurant, who was as keen as I was to get a move on with the ordering, started yelling. Into his cell phone.

"If you're *serious* about your recovery," he was saying, "you'll turn this over to your higher power. You know what I'm saying?" He walked back and forth, listened, shaking his head. "Screw that shit, man! Let go and let God. That bitch girlfriend can take care a herself. She ain't worth two sticks rubbed together."

He slammed his cell phone shut and stood, arms crossed, scowling at magenta jumpsuit lady who was still trying to count her money.

"It's sixteen forty-five," the clerk said.

"'K, then, um, that's too much, too much. I need two dollars. Take off one a them Boston Cremes is all you need to do." She shuffled through the words.

"Oh, Lord," the clerk said. She rolled her eyes. "You know I already rang it up. Now you making me go and write up an over-ring? Again?"

"I just don't have enough," the lady said.

I peered over magenta lady's shoulder, counted her money myself. The cashier wasn't helping.

"You have eighteen dollars," I snapped. "Do I need to count it for you?"

The guy on the cell phone looked at me, eyes big as breakfast plates. It was as if he was seeing me for the first time. He looked down at my feet for a couple seconds.

"Hey man, what kinda boots are those?" he asked me.

"I have no idea," I said. I glanced down. My go-go boots shone in the overhead lights. I'd spit-shined them on my way out. The rhinestones sparkled.

"You could kick some serious ass with those big boots," he said. "What size are they? You got some big mother-fucking feet." I wasn't sure if the guy was paying me a compliment; I'd never heard of anybody kicking ass with go-go boots, but I figured what he really meant was something like "big feet, big you-know-what." It wasn't the first time somebody'd cruised me at the Krispy Kreme.

"Look," I implored, to nobody in particular, my arms out, crucifixion-style, "all I want is a cup of coffee!"

"I'm really sorry," the clerk said, peering around magenta jumpsuit lady, "but I can't take any orders 'til this customer gives me sixteen forty-five. Gotta complete the transaction."

The cute guy got back on his cell phone, started up again with the person he'd been talking to the first time around.

"Well, did you tell her?" he asked, then paused. "Look, man, the same Jesus that took care a you is gonna take care a her. You'll be all right soon as you push that cracked-out, sorry-ass bitch through the door. Just do it, man." He looked around the restaurant, then caught a load of my feet. "There's this dude here at the Krispy Kreme's with some big-ass lady's boots, and it got me thinking about those shoe ads and how they say 'Just do it.' Just put that bitch on the street, man. Just do it. Let go and let God." He slammed the phone shut again. "Just do it!" he yelled to the place, sounding like a preacher on Sunday morning.

In the back, I could see through the order window, see the baker leave her conveyor belt of donuts; she stuck her head out the side door to see who was making all the commotion in the restaurant. She looked at me and went back to sorting, shaking her head as she threw hot donuts in boxes.

"All's I need is forty-five cents," magenta-jumpsuit lady was saying. "Who's got forty-five cents?" I was mad now— the damn lady *couldn't* count.

"I do!" I said. "I'll pitch in two bucks, if it gets me coffee."

"Now hold on, just a sec," the cell phone guy interrupted, his hand on my shoulder, pulling me to face him. The cashier glowered at the near miss, the cash *interruptus*. Cell phone guy lowered his voice. "Figure she's strung out?"

"Yep," I said.

"Now, a minute ago, I thought you were some kinda kick-ass dude, when you told that bitch to pay for her donuts. But you know, it's not gonna help if you pay for her food. It's called *enabling*."

"*Hell-ooo,*" I said, rapping my knuckles against my own forehead. "How long you been clean?"

"Been nine months," he said. He had nothing on me. I turned away.

And with that, the front doors to the place swung open and a cold wind swept in. A teenage boy sauntered up to magenta jumpsuit lady. He wore a stained "Tupac—RIP" T-shirt, and his glasses sat on the end of his nose. One of the lenses had a lightning-shaped crack running through.

"Mama," he said, "what's goin' on?"

"*Oooh,* I'm trying to pay for these *goddamn* donuts," she hollered, "but I need forty-five *motherfucking* cents!" She held her head high, like a dog bellowing at the moon.

Her boy peered at the floor, embarrassed, and shuffled his feet in his mismatched bedroom slippers; he sighed, and his breath, its sound so soft, yet so audible, overtook the entire restaurant, as if a wind from some underworld had blown right through. I knew that sigh. I remembered it. Something knocked at me.

"I'll pay for your food," I heard myself saying. "Have anything you want." Cell phone guy glared at me.

"It's sixteen forty-five, then," the clerk said. The boy looked down again. His mother shook her head wildly, "No, no, no, no," and thrummed her fingers on the counter. She would not turn to look at me.

"Mama, just let him pay and let's get on home." She slumped. I paid. "Thank you, sir."

The boy kept his eyes down, and they stuffed a dispenser full of napkins into their box of donuts. As the doors swung closed behind them, I finally got to order my coffee. Cell phone guy ignored me, stood way over to the side over by the half-and-half containers and stir rods and Sweet 'N Lows.

"That was a nice thing you did, hon. Need anything else?" The clerk asked me softly, her tone different now. She touched her hand to mine for a moment.

"Huh?"

"You're … crying," she whispered, pointing her long gold nail to her cheek. She slipped a napkin across the counter with some sugar packets.

I wasn't tasting my weak coffee as I turned and watched magenta jumpsuit lady and her son slip into their car, their box of free donuts steaming on the seat between them. Their old car thumped around the corner, and I kept my gaze fixed for a long while, fixed on the window and on my own wavy reflection in the glass.

Waiting on the
Nuthatches' Arrival

The dishwasher dial creaks. It labors through mechanized cleaning, while inside, the cups tinkle, dance to whooshing water jets. I feel stuck in place, all right, like someone brooding as they shoot glances down the track for a late train. I'm just passing Grandfather's time. He has Alzheimer's, and when I stay with him, I am alone, too. Just out of school, I'm the only person in my family on hand for duty, so I sit with him for the pocket change that they pay me. All day, I sit and gaze at Grandfather's back yard through plate glass, peer at the blond leaves on the trees, the yellow decay all dotted with variegated sunlight.

I sit here and wonder: How do I address this old man who told me so many times that I wasn't "up to snuff"? I always believed him, and now I listen for him as he naps in his chair, hope to hear absolution or even some acceptance. I only get occasional snorts or mumbling gestures or laughs at some ghost's joke from the past.

When he wakes (which isn't often), he'll try to tell me something, speaking with a clumsy tongue. And when he does talk, his old intonation, the diction, is still there. Sometimes I pretend he is the same artist he always was, the strokes and hues of his voice unchanged. Now, though, the words don't come in sentences; they only splatter the canvas of language. Today, he gets frustrated with himself, shakes his arms, slaps his thighs, tries to get the words right so he'll see my face spark and light with understanding. I fake it, pretend to know what the hell he's talking about. I nod and smile. What else can I do?

I hold a glass for him.

"Grandfather, sip this water. The doctor wants you to." I hold the green straw, hope he'll notice it—green's his favorite color. He falls asleep again, his jaw slackening like a used-up rubber band.

During this stretch of the day, the clock (a grandfather clock—the irony does not go unnoticed) nags with its timekeeping. It chimes and *tick-tick-ticks,* disturbs the old man sometimes and wakes him. I need some peace without meanness—the old man's moods get especially bad late in the day. I stop the clock so it won't bother him, hold its brass pendulum until the ticking ends, bar it from swinging or telling time. Ah, silence. Then I check the hour, just in case, on my watch. It's three-thirty. I wonder what would happen if I moved the clock hands backwards.

Outside, on the brick patio, I've strewn some seeds out there for the birds; they pepper the slippery moss and lichen. Every day at four o'clock, the birds, mostly nuthatches, swoop down in groups; they are tiny, resolute in their feeding. I glance at my watch again. Three thirty-five p.m. They'll be here, as always, at four.

Grandfather wakes, motions to the bathroom, and I prop him on the toilet, slip his underwear to his ankles, and crack the door, leave him alone, lend some privacy, then I help with pads and flushing, but only if he asks. I remind him, "Don't forget to wash your hands."

He pushes his walker; it clicks and slides as he searches for his bedroom. It's down the hall. He goes the wrong way. I let him—he needs the exercise. And so, he laps the house again and again, panting, looking for something familiar. In the living room, he steals knickknacks off his own coffee table and chuckles at his childlike ingenuity. He stashes the booty in the patch pocket of his robe; he doesn't remember that I gave him the malachite egg for Christmas '89, or that Aunt Maggie gave him the fish paperweight years ago. He's thieving his own possessions and shushes me when I watch him. He lifts a crooked finger to his lips. *Shhhh!*

"Don't tell," he commands. Later, I'll slip everything from his pockets and put them back. He'll steal them again tomorrow and the next day.

Finally, he finds his chair and plops down, and I fetch the quilt Grandmother made decades ago, every stitch a labor of his wife's love.

"You're bruising me. Don't touch me." I let him fuss at me, tuck the quilt under his knees, the way he likes, careful, tight.

"Is this chair new? It's real nice." He runs his hand across the arm, smoothing blue velvet pile, and I grin.

"It is nice, isn't it?" He's had the chair five years.

Today, like every other day, I sit beside him and wait. I wait for acceptance. I wait for his breathing to slow again into sleep. I wait for the nuthatches' arrival at four o'clock. And I wait for the last cycle on the dishwasher, so I can put all his dishes away.

Objects in Mirror
Are Closer Than They Appear

Is there always a hard way to go home?
—Eudora Welty

Today, Frank Hardin's wife, Birdie, needed sneakers. At the mall, in the sporting goods store, he watched her tie on every shoe from the clearance rack, jamming her puffy feet into white, perforated leather or into shiny pink nylon or even black patent joggers, checking each pairs' fit in the slanted floor mirrors stationed next to the tennis rackets, the sports jerseys, the golf clubs. His face prickled hot as she squatted and jumped, squatted and jumped, over and over. Well, yes, he thought, she *had* ballooned bigger, with those thin ankles and that large middle, as if she'd topple over with one gentle push. As pliant as a sleeping cow.

His shame was his alone. As she bent her knees, dipping and lunging, standing on her tiptoes in her prospective shoes, tender feelings welled up as he watched her old black purse sway on her wrist like a pendulum; the shredded strap had been sewn and repaired so many times.

"I like these the best. But maybe they're a little snug," she complained, screwing up her face in pain.

"They'll stretch after use," he said, impatient.

"But I really think they're too tight."

"No, no, dear, the leather'll stretch, I tell you."

"Well, if you say so," she said, "you know best … I'll wait for you outside." Her voice faded as if she'd come to the end of a song. With the red *SALE!* price tag still stuck to her left sole, she walked out of the store, waited by the spewing fountain for him to pay.

Upstairs, he and Birdie stood right in the doorway of the expensive lingerie place that sent all those catalogs in the mail. It reeked of strong perfume and money.

"Too rich for our blood, Frank." Birdie pushed him right along. "Anyway, give me a month with this new workout."

So they walked on over to the Klothes Korral, a discount store at the back of the mall. And they found some panties on one of the sale tables, leopard-print French-cuts that fit Birdie's behind. They were $2.14 with tax. He didn't even have to use his credit card. He just flipped the money from his clip.

In the car, his scowl softened. Saturdays were good. He always had a project on Saturdays. It was the weekdays; those were the days that sunk him. Damned *retirement:* the worst word in the English language.

Now, driving home, their errands accomplished, he wasn't feeling any of the usual weight of uselessness. The four-lane road's stitched yellow lines flew by. And his tight, narrow shoulders eased back farther in his seat.

He chose the turnoff to the long, scenic route home. He looked over at Birdie.

"Spent the nest egg, practically." He chuckled, proud of the money they'd saved, his bony hands loose on the steering wheel. Birdie dozed, didn't respond; her new shoes were kicked off on the floorboard, and the old ones thrown on the backseat like forgotten toys. The panties were back there, too, in a plastic bag next to her purse. He glanced over at her again; her head rested to the side, and she made peeping noises, little wet air sounds out her nose. He checked his side-view mirror, and instead of looking for cars to his left, he noted the etched lettering in caps along the bottom: "OBJECTS IN MIRROR ARE CLOSER THAN THEY APPEAR." Did that mean they were closer in life or in the mirror? Why did they have make everything so confusing?

He drove and meandered, wove in and out, skirted tow trucks and taxis, SUVs, as they passed all the columned houses, all the places with their straight rows of trees and hedges, their wide, straight drives. Success was everywhere, even in the lofty scent of mown grass he whiffed through his half-open window. The light canted, cast shadows on all the majestic brick mailboxes. Every house had a brick mailbox.

"You're snoring. Breathe through your mouth," he reminded Birdie, then clicked on the radio. He whistled along to some old song with its tinny string section and thought he heard Birdie humming, too.

"Almost home." He whispered the words, not sure if he were really talking anyone now. The houses in their own subdivision were small in stature, huddled together, overwhelmed by the wide-open spaces of the large county surrounding them. Small bushes, poorly pruned, round or square, dotted the yards. And the spindly mailboxes that waited at the curbs were all stuck in the ground like crooked toothpicks.

When he pulled into their cul-de-sac, the streetlights were brightening. Yes, there it was. Their own brick mailbox. He'd built it himself, mixing the perfect shade of gray mortar, searching for the right dusty hue of red for the bricks.

Inside, he found a cold one on the refrigerator door, then switched on the game. When Birdie slammed the back door, he heard the laundry room door creak, the dial click on the washer, the water swoosh into the machine.

He awoke to the sound of Birdie crying.

"They're ruined!" Birdie stood over him, nudged his shoulder, as she came in close. In both her hands, she cupped the new leopard print panties. She pushed them at him like an offering. Though there wasn't much left to offer.

"They ruined in the wash," she sniffed. He could see that as he gazed at the light brown lump no more than a piece of wet string and elastic and mushy fabric. Even the leopard brown spots had vanished. Birdie placed them on the his chair arm, then pulled the sheers across the drape rod, *shuuuuusssssh.*

"Did you save the receipt?" he asked.

"It's right here. Wish I could've worn those." She said it as if she meant it, with half a smile, then shuffled off to the kitchen.

The panties and receipt sat there in a bulge on the arm of his chair. The receipt with the words, "All sales final." He'd see about that.

Dinner was another meal of solitude between them. After scraping down the plates, Birdie stood up, started the dishwasher, started on the pots in the sink. She turned and smiled at him as he sat at the table. He watched as her eyes drifted past to the window where her gaze stuck on a dead, dangling bumblebee in a spiderweb. He folded and refolded his cloth napkin. Life with Birdie wasn't too bad if he doled out little bits of affection, showed appreciation— in the hall, a peck on the cheek, or, while she washed dishes, a pat on the behind. And with odd jobs attended to—her, working in the kitchen, hands red from scrubbing; him, in the garage puttering about—life was good.

Frank sat at the table while she watched her favorite TV show, and, once in a while, he could hear her from the living room, yelling at the tube—"You don't buy a vowel, not yet!" or "It's Betty Crocker, you dolt, that's easy!" or "I tell you, Vanna."

He shuffled upstairs, turned out lights as he went and found Birdie deep in her dreams. He watched her for a moment. She slept with her mouth agape, the drool collecting on her green pillowcase in a spot the shape of

Florida. Her eyes twitched under parted lids. She mumbled something, then rolled over with her back to him. If he squinted real hard, she wasn't his lumpy wife anymore, but the young thing he'd met back when. He couldn't get enough of her then and those smooth legs the color of toast, the way they wrapped around his waist. He slid in.

"Night." Birdie turned to him, mumbled and touched his thigh, smacked her lips together as if he'd said something appetizing.

"I tell you Birdie, I'll get that money for those panties. It's not right, you know?" He often talked to her when she was sleeping. All his secrets, he waited to tell them all until she was dreaming. Everything had already seemed stored up in her; Birdie, plump and pretty, was bloated with all she knew and hoarded.

He kissed her neck, then ran a hand under her nightgown. Compliant, she slipped sideways under him as a mechanic might slide under the body of a car. She spread her legs, and he hiked up her gown over her full hips, caressed the soft skin there between her thighs. He thought about all the other people all over the world doing this same thing at that exact moment, too. It was life's code, a message unspoken, but one he understood somehow.

"I'm gonna get that money back, Birdie. They cheated us, that's what they did. They outright cheated us."

"Umm-hmm. That's nice. You do that," she replied, her voice distant, as if she were tipping some bagboy at the grocery. He ran his fingers down her spine and rested them on her warm thigh swaddled inside the flannel nightgown, and then fell into a fitful sleep.

A couple hours of watching the clock and Frank was anxious. He gulped down coffee as he sat under the découpaged "Bless This Mess" plaque. It was still early. At ten forty-five, he stuffed the receipt and panties in his jacket.

"I'd go, Frank," Birdie said, "but I've got Sunday dinner to fix." She was already outfitted in her exercise clothes, her new shoes blazing white. She clanked a Dutch oven to the sink from some overhead cabinet and began swirling soapy water around in it.

Birdie came onto the stoop and watched him drive off. She shielded her face from the sun with a chunky hand and frowned. On the drive to the mall, he found Sunday morning traffic slow, with all those gray-haired cronies in their big, white American cars heading home from church. He parked at the mall and waited outside the store on a bench. A fountain behind him smelled of chlorine and spurted water into plumes; its splashes echoed off the tile courtyard, and pennies, thrown with small wishes, flashed in the shallow pool. Pink, waxy flowers thrived in black plastic planters. And all the stores' cash registers hummed with predatory speed as they prepared for the day's sales. Frank's face was on fire.

At two minutes to noon, the Klothes Korral's gate went up. The doors clicked with a turn of a bolt. The clerk inside, who looked him over and smiled as he entered, made her way up to the register. Frank followed. She wore an orange sweater, stretched tight over her chest, her nipples hard as lug nuts under the fuzzy fabric.

"Hold on, just a sec," she said and bent over to hit a switch. He checked out her firm bottom. The pink neon lights on the back wall buzzed, then glowed. She stood in a flood of rosy neon light and tucked a stray hair behind her ear.

"I need to return these. They fell apart in the wash." He handed her the panties and the receipt. She held up the slip of paper and frowned, and his face burned even hotter as she pushed the shredded panties on the counter with the tip of a pencil.

"Well, sir, as you can see, it's clearly printed on the receipt. 'All sales final.'" She tapped the receipt on the counter with her long silver nail, then pushed the panties again with the pencil point and wrinkled her nose. "And no one takes underwear returns! It's not hygienic!" She turned away and clicked on the store stereo. The music on the sound system pumped out a distorted sound as if the music were underwater. His head was thrumming. Sweat ran in streams under his armpits, trailed across his stomach.

"You will. Take these." He gulped his words. "These fell apart in the wash. Faulty manufacturing. Where's your manager?"

"I am the manager. All sales are final. Sorry." She turned her back and started sorting price tags. Something swelled inside him like a sponge.

"Damned fool!" he screamed, then lobbed the panties at a speaker. They crinkled down to the floor and sat in a muddy brown clump on the carpet.

The sales clerk glowered; her right hand found the phone receiver.

"I'm calling security."

"Fool!" He screamed it again as he snatched up the wounded looking panties, stuffed them into his pants pocket. He stormed the door, pulled blouses off their hangers as he stomped his way, tossing sweaters off display shelves. When he reached the mouth to the mall, he threw his hands in the air like he was pitching confetti at a party.

He pushed his way through the crowds, through the food court, nudging past the curly fries and the frosted oranges, past the noodles-in-a-cup, gyros, and two-minute tacos, and jostled through the lines in the food court.

Outside, the trees were so bare he could spot mistletoe in the branches and fallen leaves scattered about the pavement in a confusion of colors. Up in the sky, buffeting clouds drifted in, wrapped themselves around the early-afternoon sun, and in the parking lot, the first raindrop spat on his bare scalp as he unlocked the door. He hit the four-lane just as the clouds broke open; the rain pelted fast. He clicked his wipers to the highest speed, but the road was a cloud of mist.

Before he knew it, his anger and hatred and the blinding rain pulled him through the distance and onto the highway. In the wrong direction. He was driving nowhere. On the radio, soft piano music was playing. Now what? The rest of the week stretched out before him—the same as last week, the same as the week before. His grip tightened on the steering wheel. He dug into his pocket and grasped the panties, then reached over and punched some dials on the radio. There was a slight twinge in his eyelid; the sponge in his head kept filling up, and his left arm contorted in a strange angle. He pulled over into the emergency lane, hit the hazards. The windshield wipers scraped and squealed as they kept rhythm with the raindrops tapping the roof. And then a roaring hit his ears. The wipers rasped on. He peered at his side mirror, finally understood the printed message along its bottom. Objects are always closer in reality.

He slipped down, twisted on his side over the console, and music from the radio reached him, a rusty flat note plucking in his chest. He grasped the panties in his fist, the fabric soft now from so much handling. And the raindrops fell a little more insistent now, their clatter resonating, tinking the roof. They rapped out a code, and the rhythm overtook him, joined the vibration inside him, and it tapped out a message unspoken, yet somehow he understood.